HOW THE HITMAN STOLE CHRISTMAS

Katie Reus

Cover art by Sweet 'N Spicy Designs
Editors: Kelli Collins and Julia Ganis
Proofreader: Book Nook Nuts
Author website: www.katiereus.com

Praise for the novels of Katie Reus

"Sexy military romantic suspense." —USA Today

"Enough sexual tension to set the pages on fire."
—*New York Times* bestselling author, Alexandra Ivy

"...a wild hot ride for readers. The story grabs you and doesn't let go."
—*New York Times* bestselling author, Cynthia Eden

"Reus strikes just the right balance of steamy sexual tension and nail-biting action....This romantic thriller reliably hits every note that fans of the genre will expect." —*Publishers Weekly*

"A sexy, well-crafted paranormal romance that succeeds with smart characters and creative world building." —Kirkus Reviews

"You'll fall in love with Katie's heroes."
—*New York Times* bestselling author, Kaylea Cross

Dedication

For all my fellow weirdos. Keep being you.

CHAPTER 1

—Sometimes I pretend to be normal, but it's boring so I go back to being me.—

One week before Christmas

Sitting in her favorite chair, Elliana stared out her favorite window. Having a favorite window was a new thing, but it was the one that gave her the perfect view of her neighbor.

Her very hot neighbor.

Who she was very much stalking.

Though she wasn't sure if it counted as stalking if he knew she was watching him with her drone and binoculars. And he definitely did. In fact, he seemed to be encouraging her.

She grabbed her cell as she stared across the yard into his open bedroom window, waiting like a total loser for him to show up. She called the first number she had saved.

"Hey, everything okay?" her friend and one of her business partners, Weston Davis, answered.

"Yeah, I just have a question. Would it be weird if I bought my hot neighbor a Christmas present?" And then casually brought it over to his place. Maybe even talked to him.

There was a long pause. "I thought he was gone."

Her hot neighbor—what she called him in her head—had been gone the last few months. Just disappeared, but he hadn't sold the house. She knew, because she'd checked. And she'd found out that the house was owned by some random corporation, which was pretty weird. But *he* was pretty weird—what kind of guy got off on letting his random neighbor watch him do stripteases? "He got back at like midnight. I saw his car pull into his garage but I haven't actually seen him yet. And you haven't answered my question. Would it be weird?"

"The whole thing you two have going on is weird. You don't even know his name!"

Not that she hadn't tried to find out. Well, she'd done everything short of actually asking him. "Oh my god, put your wife on the phone!"

There was a brief rustling, then Rebel Martinez—yes, *that* Rebel, freaking global musical superstar—came on the line. "Hey, bestie! Why'd you call Weston first?"

"He was the first person on my saved contacts, but you're right. I'll never be calling him for advice again because he's terrible at it. I know you heard, so what should I do?"

"What kind of gift are you thinking of getting him?"

Elliana wasn't going to admit that she'd sort of already bought him a gift. "I was thinking some of the coffee he likes. It's super fancy and special order. He also eats these little Scottish biscuits every morning." Well, the mornings he was at his house.

"Ooh, that's so cute. But can you explain to me why you haven't talked to him yet?"

"I don't know. I saw him move in one day and accidentally spied on him in his bedroom. He saw my little drone and gave me a strip show. I have no idea how to talk to him now! It's too weird." And she never had problems talking to men. She'd been a Marine, after all. But this was different—she very much wanted to have sex with her hot neighbor. Just sex. Hopefully more than once. To get him out of her system once and for all.

She didn't *do* relationships—life had taught her that people couldn't be trusted. At least, hot people with penises. They lied because they could, and they hurt people they were supposed to care for. Ugh. But that didn't stop her from obsessing over her neighbor with the sculpted jaw and annoyingly adorable dimples.

"I still don't know what to think about it. Does he, like...bring other women home? Do you watch?"

"Rebel!" Weston said in the background, his horror clear.

Elliana ignored him. "Uh, hell no. I wouldn't watch that." It made her irrationally jealous even thinking about him with other women. Her nameless, gorgeous neighbor. Damn it, she really did need to talk to him. AKA bang his brains out. "But I do watch other things." Like him masturbating for her sometimes. She kept that to herself, however.

"Oh, I have a pretty good idea what 'other things' means. So the good news is that he's just as weird as you. Which means you've got nothing to worry about. Just walk next door and give him the gift I *know* you already bought."

Elliana could hear Weston groaning in the background about how this was terrible advice. But what did he know? "Fine, I *have* already bought it. And I made a cute little gift basket and everything." Even though she hated Christmas, she'd made an exception for the ripped hottie next door.

And she felt stupid thinking the word hottie, but she wasn't sure how else to describe him. The man sometimes did workouts in addition to the strip shows he put on for her. Sometimes he did pull-ups on a bar he'd set up in the doorway of the bedroom. And it was perfectly visible from her second-story window.

Over and over, he pulled that hard body up and down. Up and down. With her drone or binos, she could see every rippling—

"Are you listening?"

Elliana blinked and pushed away from her chair. She needed to stop this obsession. "Yeah, sorry."

"Well then?"

"Well...what?" Elliana asked.

"Oh my god, I knew you weren't listening. You still haven't RSVP'd to our Christmas Eve party."

Oh right. She wasn't doing any dumb Christmas parties. Not even with people she loved. "I can't hear you. Oh, I'm going through a tunnel, gotta go." She hung up in the middle of Rebel's protests as she headed downstairs to her kitchen.

She glared at the cutesy red-and-white gift basket on her countertop. It was the only Christmas-themed thing in her house. She stared some more, frowned at the innate cheerfulness of the gift, then rolled her eyes at herself.

"Just do it," she growled into the quiet of her kitchen. "Give him the gift, then see if he wants to unwrap you."

She snatched the basket up off the countertop, then made her way to her front door. After turning off her alarm, she slipped on sandals and stepped out into the slightly chilly air. Christmastime in Miami usually meant light-sweater weather, but there was a nip in the air that made her consider going upstairs to grab some real shoes.

But no—if she went back inside, she'd never get the courage to do this again.

With determined strides, she made her way to the sidewalk, turned left, then made the short distance to her neighbor's walkway. She eyed all the Christmas decorations he'd hired some company to put up while he'd been out of town.

He was beyond sexy, so she could forgive the whole love of Christmas thing.

Tension built at the back of her neck as she made her way up to his front door—that had a stupid-looking snowman cutout smiling at her.

"This is a dumb idea," she muttered to herself, paused, thought about going home, then forced herself onward. She needed to meet this guy once and for all and find out if he was worth actually talking to. If he wasn't, she was going to stop spying on her neighbor.

Probably.

She rang the doorbell, then waved at the little doorbell camera. Then she inwardly cursed herself. God, could she be more pathetic? She'd never actually asked a guy out before. Normally they hit on her. A lot. But for some reason, this guy had decided to put on sexy shows for her instead of approaching. Maybe she should just leave well enough alone.

After twenty seconds with no response, she realized he wasn't coming to the door. Probably for the best. She set the present down and had started to turn away from the door when she heard the snick of the dead bolt releasing.

Elliana turned, and as her neighbor opened the door, all the breath left her lungs in a whoosh. It should seriously be illegal to look so good. Totally illegal.

His dark hair was slightly rumpled, and without his shirt on—truly, the man seemed to be allergic to clothes—his biceps looked even bigger as he held the door open. He did that "hot guy" pose where he had one hand up on the frame as he smiled at her, revealing those dimples.

Dimples!

"Hey, Elliana." He sounded all breathless and that made her think so many things.

Dirty, naked things.

Oh wait, he knew her name? That was weird...or maybe not. She *had* been on the cover of *Forbes*, though not everyone read that. Or maybe he'd found out from one of their neighbors? She cleared her throat. "Hey. Uh..." She shoved the basket at him, was glad when he took it from her. "I brought you a Christmas gift."

His grin widened and those dimples sent ribbons of heat curling through her, warming her up from the inside out. Oh, this was so bad.

So very bad.

"I didn't think you celebrated." He chin nodded to her yard. "You're the only one in the neighborhood without decorations." Even his voice was addicting, deep, dark and sort of rumbly. Oh, so rumbly.

She lifted a shoulder, feeling awkward and hating it. In her experience, men usually weren't complex. But this guy had her all twisted up. "I've been working a lot." She mumbled the lie. She *never* decorated. But he hadn't lived in the neighborhood long enough to realize that.

"I've got some extra decorations. Maybe I can put them up for you?" His pale amber eyes that had always reminded her of a tiger's dipped to her mouth as he spoke.

And she found herself staring at his mouth now, watching that full bottom lip as he talked. Before she could respond, there was a thud from inside his house.

Oh, hell, was he not alone? Of course he wasn't. She felt so stupid. This guy might give her strip shows but of course he wasn't like celibate or anything. She took a step backward. "Well, I hope you enjoy the present."

He stepped out, his jogging pants riding low on his hips, showing off a faint trail of dark hair pointing downward. As if she needed any help figuring out where the good stuff was. The outline of his package was very, very clear.

Stop, stop, stop. She had to stop this obsession with him.

"It's my dog," he said, stepping out onto the porch, reaching for her.

Maybe she'd lost her mind because she didn't actually care when he loosely grasped her wrist. Not when a spark of heat jolted through her. "You have a dog?"

"Just got him," he said, but she could tell he was lying.

"Uh huh. Look, whatever you do in your own home is your business. I'm just being neighborly." *Lies, lies, lies.* She absolutely didn't want to think about what he'd been doing before she'd shown up. Why had he even answered the door if he'd been hooking up with someone? "I hope you have a good Christmas."

"Wait—"

The sound of a groan came from inside. A very distinctive groaning of someone in pain.

Without thought, she shoved past him and hurried inside—and stared as a bloody man tried to crawl across the foyer toward the front door. He tried to rasp something out through the gag in his mouth as Elliana continued to stare in horror.

At the sound of the door clicking shut behind her, she turned and found her hot neighbor holding a gun on her.

Sighing, he tossed her a pair of flex cuffs. "I really wish you hadn't seen that. Put those on your wrists and secure yourself to..." He looked around, nodded at a column by a nearly empty dining room. This house didn't even look lived in. All the furniture was clearly staged and there were no photos or personal touches anywhere. *What the hell?*

Heart racing, she moved over to one of the nineties-era columns and wrapped her arms around it and started to secure her wrists. For a brief moment, she thought about fighting him, but he was huge and he looked incredibly comfortable holding that SIG.

Damn it. She could fight, sure, but she didn't know enough about him to try to attack just yet. Not to mention, she wasn't bulletproof or faster than a damn bullet. Rushing him when all his attention was on her would be monumentally stupid. She'd have to be patient and wait for the right time.

"Why'd you even answer the door?" she demanded as she pulled the flex ties tighter, even as she fought the fear punching through her. He could have just ignored her at the door! And avoided this whoooole kidnapping thing. Oh, she was going to kick his ass once she got free.

"I didn't want to miss my chance to talk to you. I didn't think this asshole would wake up though. Hey, not too tight, I don't want you to hurt yourself." Concern laced his voice as he approached. As he did, he released the magazine and showed her that his weapon was empty. Then he checked the flex ties and frowned, as if they offended him. As if he hadn't ordered her to put them on!

"Wait, your SIG was empty?" she asked through gritted teeth.

He looked affronted—actually offended!—that she could even ask. "I would never pull a loaded weapon on you."

"Says the man who has me tied up and is clearly torturing some other guy," she snapped.

Hot Neighbor glanced over at the still groaning bloody guy. The man was restrained, and he'd been worked over good. Had bruises forming all over his ribs and back.

"He deserved it. He hurts kids and thinks he can get away with it." Now his voice was a low, angry rumble as he glared down at his bloody victim. "But he's going to tell me the names of his perverted friends, and then I might end his life quickly." Then he turned back to Elliana, his expression shifting. "I'm really sorry you walked in on this."

Elliana blinked at him. "I *knew* you were a psychopath!" Of course he was. Her man radar was broken beyond repair, always had been.

He lifted a dark, imperious eyebrow, and damn it, looked so good doing it. "Says the woman who's been watching me with her drone for the better part of the year."

"You didn't have to put on strip shows for me! Or...masturbate." She whispered the last part for some reason and cursed the way her cheeks heated up. She'd been pretty sure she was past blushing at this point, but apparently not.

"You liked it."

Yep, she sure had, but she wasn't going to tell him that when she was tied up and wondering if he was going to kill her next. Man, she really did have terrible taste in men. Like epically catastrophic. And she had no one to blame but herself. Not when she'd walked over here willingly to give him a gift based solely on how attractive he was. *Damn it!*

"Look, I'll be right back and we'll talk this out. I swear this isn't what it seems." He kicked the guy when he groaned before hoisting him up as if he weighed nothing. "I mean, it is what it seems in that I'm *definitely* killing him. But he's an evil piece of shit and I'm not sorry about this. The world will be a better place without him in it. Give me a couple minutes to secure him, and then we're going to talk."

Once again, all she could do was stare as her neighbor strode out of the dining room and went deeper into his house. When she heard a door thud shut, she slammed the flex ties—and unfortunately her wrists—against the column over and over until they snapped free.

A little trick she'd learned years ago. If you hit them just right, the snap broke.

Ignoring the jolt of pain in her arms, she ran to the door, unlocked it and raced out of this house. She sprinted across her front lawn, not stopping until she was in her house and had the dead bolt in place.

Then she set her alarm and raced upstairs to grab her own weapon. And unlike him, hers had a full magazine loaded.

Once she was armed, she grabbed her cell phone and started to call the police.

But...her finger paused over the emergency button.

No, dammit. She needed to call them.

It would be the logical thing to do.

Yes, definitely normal.

But she *had* recognized the bloody guy from the floor, remembered seeing his face on the news. He'd been on trial for raping his daughter's friend but was let go for some insane reason. The jury had found that the girl—who was only seventeen—had come on to him or some bullshit. Please. The guy was human garbage. Still...

"Do it," she ordered herself.

But in the end, she put her phone aside, even as she questioned her own sanity.

CHAPTER 2

—My life is unpredictable,
but my bad choices are a constant.—

Elliana had spent the last twenty-four hours inside her house *not* calling the police.

Not doing anything except spying on her murderous neighbor's house. And trying to figure out who the hell he was. She hadn't done a deep dive before for reasons she didn't want to examine too closely—namely, trying not to violate his privacy with her hacking skills.

Now she had no choice.

Unfortunately, there were too many layers for her to sift through.

She could run his face through a facial recognition program she shouldn't have access to, but part of her was worried that it might trigger something at Interpol or any number of agencies. The guy was a freaking killer. An unapologetic one at that.

He had to be wanted or on some kind of list. And against her better judgment, she didn't want to turn him in just yet. Or maybe at all.

Ugh.

Something was wrong with her, she acknowledged as she quietly eased up the Roman shade in the guest room where she normally spied from. She'd kept it down all day and night and just used her drone and cameras to watch his house.

He'd left in his car at one point—likely to dispose of the body, which was no doubt wrapped up in his trunk—but then he'd come back and he'd had the balls to wave at one of her cameras. Then wink at her! As if he didn't have a care in the world.

His confidence was as annoying as it was sexy. Maybe she should be turned off that he was a killer, but she'd killed too. Though it had been in a different capacity. When she'd been in the Marines, she'd been an explosives expert—was still an expert, thank you very much.

And she'd researched the guy he'd killed last night. To say he'd deserved death was an understatement. That piece of shit had raped his daughter's best friend, a girl he'd known since she was a child. He'd used her trust in him to hurt her in the worst way possible. Then he'd made it look like she'd come on to him. But after he'd been found not guilty, more evidence had come to light that he'd used burner phones to fake messages between them. And that he'd hurt more than just his daughter's friend, because of course he had.

There was currently an arrest warrant out for him on multiple counts of so many horrific things Elliana didn't even want to think about, issued yesterday.

Too little too late. And unfortunately for the cops, they weren't ever going to find him. Or not alive, anyway.

That was why she didn't call the cops. Well, one of the reasons—the second reason she couldn't even think about right now. She'd seen the shit the world had to offer, and for her it had always existed in shades of gray. What her neighbor did was wrong, sure, but she wasn't going to lose any sleep over his actual crime. And...she wasn't scared of him. He hadn't even pulled a loaded weapon on her.

Damn it, now she was rationalizing everything.

She nearly jumped back when she realized he was staring out of his own window, watching, clearly waiting for her.

Shirtless.

What was it with him and running around in no clothes? His hair looked damp and tousled and he held up a cup of coffee as he smiled at her. Just smiled cheekily, showing off those dimples that made her knees all wobbly—even though he'd just tortured a human being to death in his house.

Yep. Something was definitely wrong with her.

Her phone buzzed in her pocket, and even though she didn't want to break eye contact first, she glanced down at it. Saw a message from a random number.

Thank you for the coffee. It's delicious.

She snapped her gaze back to him and he nodded at her, pointed to the phone she now saw in his hand. How the hell did he have her phone number?

Angrily, she typed back. *How'd you get my number?* Because she literally worked in security and privacy; was one of the co-founders of a new up-and-coming company that had gone public over a year ago. Which meant her net worth had gone up considerably—not that she'd moved or changed her spending habits. She liked her life the way it was, liked her neighborhood and all her neighbors—though she had serious reservations about this one—even if they were bonkers about Christmas. Her friend Van had recently told her that she was just afraid of change, but what did he know?

Alice from two doors down gave it to me. I told her I wanted to help you decorate for Christmas and she practically shoved it at me. He grinned when he looked back up at her. Then he typed, *I'm coming over.*

She looked over at him, but he'd already turned away. Her fingers flew across the screen furiously. *No! No, no, no.*

Yep. See you in a few. You look really sexy in that green sweater. Though everything you wear is sexy.

Frowning at the screen, she hurried out into the hallway and downstairs. No, this wasn't happening. She simply wouldn't open the door, that was all.

Angry at herself, she grabbed her own SIG, tucked it in the back of her pants, then retrieved the Taser she kept in her living room. She pulled up her doorbell video and turned on the audio function. He was already standing on her doorstep. "You need to leave."

"Nope. I figured since the cops never showed up, you didn't narc me out. Which means I've still got a chance with you. I'd like to take you out to breakfast."

A *chance*? After he'd just tortured someone to death?

"Are you crazy?" Angry, she yanked open her front door and held out her Taser in one hand. She kept it low enough that some of her neighbors who were out walking their dogs couldn't see it. It was Friday and all the kids were on holiday break, so the neighborhood was busier than normal.

He simply grinned that panty-melting grin, damn him. "Probably a little. So can I take you out to breakfast?"

"I already ate. And this is a stupid conversation. Because we're not going anywhere. We shouldn't even be talking. *You* should be behind bars." *Should he really?* that little voice in her head asked. The one that hated how much women and kids were hurt every single day. And this guy had killed a known abuser. The world was a better place, and if she was being really honest, she wasn't afraid of her neighbor. Even if she should be.

He shrugged. "Probably. Thank you again for this coffee. I didn't get to properly thank you."

"It's no big deal." Why was she still standing here talking to him?

"Oh, but it is. I know you had to special order this, which means you were definitely thinking about me."

"Don't flatter yourself." Ugh. *Good one, Elliana,* she chided herself. It was like she forgot how to talk around him.

"I think about you too. All the time," he murmured, his voice dipping lower than it already was. There was heat and intent in his pale amber eyes and in his voice.

And oh, that rumble of his words reverberated through her. So bad. This was so, sooooo bad.

"If I can't take you to breakfast," he continued, "maybe I can take you to lunch? Or make you lunch?" His eyes heated even more. "Or make you come."

Her Taser hand wavered slightly. "What?"

"With my mouth. Or fingers? Or..." He smiled that devastating smile. "Any part of me you'd like. You are free to use me any way you choose."

Holy baby Jesus. "There is something seriously wrong with you!" She liked it better when she'd been spying on him and he hadn't said anything. He'd just been this hot guy who took off his clothes for her. Which, okay, even thinking that was weird. But whatever! Things had gotten way too real with him, and that wasn't even considering the whole *murder* thing.

"I know. My dad tells me that all the time."

"You have a dad?"

"Well I wasn't spawned."

She snorted in disbelief. "So you just want to pretend that..." She glanced around the neighborhood. Even though it was nine in the morning and a few of her neighbors were out, it wasn't like they could overhear them. "You didn't do what you did last night?" She didn't want to spell the words out.

"I believe in honesty, at least with you. And like I said, he deserved it." His expression went dark for a moment, even as he continued. "I only hurt people who hurt others."

She...found that she believed him. And that terrified her. "I don't even know your name."

"It's Theo Contos. And I know you're Elliana Reed." He was still smiling at her like a total weirdo. A really hot weirdo with dimples and muscles for days.

"This conversation is over. And I'm not going to lunch with you. Just...go away." She stepped back and slammed the door in his face. Then set her dead bolt. Her heart was racing out of control as she leaned against the door, trying not to picture his stupidly handsome face.

And that smile. Not charming, because she hated charming.

It was just...warm and inviting.

Which made no sense, considering he was a straight-up killer. But she'd been around killers before. The remorseless kind. Back when she'd been in the Marines, she and her team had been paired up with a black ops group on two different occasions. And those guys...they'd been the kind of killers she'd had nightmares about.

Theo wasn't like that. Or she didn't think he was.

The doorbell on her app went off and, against her better judgment, she pulled it up on her phone, saw his face smiling at her on-screen. "I'm picking you up at noon. There's a place we can walk to from here. Only a few minutes away." He named one of her favorite restaurants.

Was that a lucky guess or did he know it was one of her favorites? "I'm not going to lunch with you."

"I'll be here at noon anyway if you change your mind." Then he tipped his mug to her and stepped off her porch, his perfect ass the best view as he headed down her walkway.

"No. No," she said to herself while he disappeared from her camera's view. "Not happening. Not going to lunch with Theo the killer. Probably not even his real name," she muttered, hurrying down the hallway on the way to her small personal gym.

She was going to pound out her frustration on her punching bag.

Because she was not—absolutely *not*—letting him take her to lunch. *Or make me come.*

Why the hell had he even offered that? Because now it was in her head and all she could think about was how amazing it would be to sit on his face.

Because clearly, she'd lost it.

CHAPTER 3

—I'm suuuper comfortable with morally gray.—

"Hey, Dad," Theo answered as he pulled out a box of Christmas stuff the decorator or whatever the hell she was, had left in the garage.

This wasn't his house, just a cover one. He used it to bring people back to when he needed a quiet place to "question" them. But then he'd seen Elliana.

And she was the only reason he'd started staying at this soulless house more.

He was still pissed that she'd walked in on that bloody piece of garbage. He'd never, in his decade of being a hitman, screwed up the way he had yesterday morning.

He hadn't secured the door to his interrogation room because he'd been so damn excited to see Elliana. That was the kind of mistake that could have gotten him killed.

But she'd finally come over to talk to him and he hadn't been about to miss the opportunity. Oh, he'd thought about talking to *her*, but he'd realized from watching her—yeah, he was totally stalking her right back—that wouldn't go over well.

She had an icy "don't screw with me" exterior that she wore like a familiar coat. It was why she was so good at her job. When she'd first started watching him with her drone, he'd thought maybe she was from a different outfit, had maybe been sent to kill him.

But after some digging, he'd realized that nope, she just liked to watch him. The hot blonde with the long legs and killer smile was a pervert. Which was perfect, because he was too. Well, only for her.

"Are you even listening to me? What are you doing?" his dad demanded as Theo grunted, dragging out one of the heavier bins into the driveway.

"I'm pulling out Christmas decorations."

"What? Why the hell are you doing that?"

"I'm going to decorate my neighbor's yard."

"What? I'm your neighbor."

"Oh, not you. The house on Sycamore. I'm decorating the house next door to it."

His dad sighed, then cursed. Loudly. "Someone's been looking into you again. Trying to figure out who owns that house you're in right now. You need to unload it and find a new place to do business."

"Oh, don't worry about that. The woman I'm going to marry is just checking up on me." And he respected that.

There was a very, very, *verrrry* long pause. "Can you repeat that?"

Theo repeated himself slowly because his dad was like sixty now. He was still a hitman too, but maybe he needed to look into hearing aids?

"So you're marrying this woman who's been stalking you?"

"I'm stalking her too. And yeah. She saw me with my 'client' last night and didn't narc on me. So now we're into the first real stages of foreplay." Or maybe it was the second stage, he wasn't sure. Because she'd been watching him masturbate for months.

"She what?" his dad shouted.

"Jesus, Dad, keep it down. You're going to give yourself a heart attack and you know Mom won't be happy if that happens. I've gotta go." He hung up before his dad could yell more. Then he popped open the bin and saw various inflatable lawn decorations. There was a snowman, a couple reindeer and a creepy-looking Grinch. He left that one and pulled out the others, started to unroll them before locating an extension cord.

Thirty minutes later, as he finished putting up the twinkling gold family of deer in front of one of Elliana's palm trees, his phone started buzzing in his pocket.

What are you doing to my lawn!? Frosty, really? I hate him!

Who the heck hates Frosty?

Me!

Grinning to himself, Theo headed back to his garage and grabbed the Grinch blow-up decoration and carried it to Elliana's yard, put him right next to a stack of sparkly presents.

This better, grinchie? he texted her, grinning over at one of her outdoor cameras. And she had a handful of them so he did a sweeping bow to a couple.

That's not even a word.

It can be your nickname.

She sent him a slew of angry-faced emojis.

Okay fine, not grinchie. How about hot stuff?

Omg, even worse!

Hmm, what about I just call you mine instead?

Aaaahhhhhhhhh! That was followed by a lot more angry-face emojis, then, *I am NOT yours.*

He grinned, then shot off one last text. *See you at twelve.* Which wasn't too long from now and he needed to shower.

After he put the bins away and shut his garage, he realized he was whistling some random Christmas tune to himself as he hurried up the stairs toward his shower. God, he was so gone for the tall, gorgeous blonde who hated Christmas.

Her eyes might be ice-blue, but whenever she looked at him they were filled with unbridled heat. Except yesterday morning, he'd seen a whole lot of anger and a little fear. Not much fear though. She'd just looked pissed and ready to take his head off for making her tie herself up.

That made him want her even more. And his woman—because soon she would be his—was all attitude along with buried rage. He wouldn't mind helping her work out whatever that rage was for the rest of his goddamn life.

With legs for days—legs he'd imagined wrapped around his waist or squeezing his head—and an ass he would absolutely worship, he had a feeling that underneath her grumpy exterior a red-hot woman burned.

All for him.

He'd never met a woman he thought could ever understand him. Understand his lifestyle. Because what he did was very much illegal in all countries. He'd essentially been raised by wolves—not literally of course, but his parents were both hitmen. Both killers. All his friends were hitmen. Or most of them anyway. Their circle was tight-knit and the chance of finding someone who wanted to be part of his life... He'd thought he'd be alone forever.

Until explosives and security expert Elliana Reed had started watching him with a whole lot more than curiosity.

By the time he'd showered and changed, his phone had started buzzing again. A smile was already pulling at his mouth as he anticipated another text from Elliana.

But what he saw made him go cold.

He reread the text from his father. Once, twice. Then he opened up the attached file.

Oh, hell no.

Plans had just changed.

CHAPTER 4

—Oh shit.—

"Hey, what's up?" Weston answered on the second ring.

"Did I call the wrong number?" Elliana looked at her screen.

"No, I've got Rebel's phone. She's currently out back playing with Lucky."

"That little terror is actually playing?" The Chihuahua was a tiny force of nature who bossed everyone around.

"More like savaging a tennis ball, but she's having fun."

"How's my baby Jupiter?" The brown and white mutt was the cutest dog ever to live and she had to actively not kidnap him every time she visited her friends' house.

"Snoozing next to me on the lanai. But I know you didn't call Rebel to talk about the dogs. Are you finally RSVPing about the party?"

She ignored the party talk. "I might be going to lunch with someone today."

"Your neighbor?"

"Yeah. Only...he's maybe a little different than I originally thought." A whole lot more murdery.

"The guy you're stalking? The one who doesn't mind... Wait, how different?"

"Um...can I talk to Rebel?" She loved Weston like a brother. That was what happened when you spent time in hellholes with someone. But she needed Rebel's opinion on this.

"What the hell is going on? What can't you tell me? Did you hack his info? Is he a criminal?"

Criminal? Oh yeah. Definitely. But her gut said he wasn't a bad guy. "I tried to hack his information."

"Wait, tried?"

"I only skimmed the surface." Because she still couldn't figure out who owned the damn house next door other than a corporation that didn't exist. Which meant that he was likely working with or for someone.

Or someones.

As in, some kind of organization.

But to what end? As a hitman? Like, did he work with other hitmen, or maybe he worked for the government? No...that didn't feel right, only because of the digging she'd done. Whoever had set up the shell corporations that owned the house and other properties had done an incredible job of hiding their tracks. So it wasn't that the setup wasn't professional. It was just that it was better than what she'd seen the CIA or NSA do. And that was... Well, it was terrifying.

"So you have no clue who this guy is?"

She sighed. "Not really."

"Don't go out with him, then."

"I..." She really shouldn't. "Okay, I won't."

There was a short pause. "Really, no arguing?"

"Nah. I need to figure out more shit before I decide what to do next." She'd just been hoping to talk to Rebel and get the go-ahead—because she'd already known Weston's advice would be all logical. *Ugh.*

"You should come over here and hang with us. And better yet, come to the damn party. Rebel is so excited and she can't believe you're not coming."

"You didn't tell her why I hate Christmas?"

"No, that's your business."

Elliana found herself oddly touched. "Oh, thanks. I...might make it, I *guess*. But I'm not making promises, and if I *do* come by for a bit, I'm not wearing any holiday crap."

"You sound like we're inviting you to an execution instead of a time for drinks and merriment. And presents!"

Rolling her eyes, she glanced down as one of her cameras triggered and saw that Theo—if that was even his real name—was putting up more inflatable decorations on her lawn. This time it was penguins. *Oh, hell no.* "Hey, I've gotta go, but I'll call you back later."

"Okay but I'm telling Rebel you RSVP'd yes, so don't disappoint her." He hung up before she could respond.

Grumbling to herself, she shoved her phone in her pocket and headed out her front door. "I'm pretty sure this constitutes harassment," she snapped as she walked around the side of the house to the area where their homes shared a fence.

"Nah, I think this is just being neighborly." Theo didn't turn around from where he was crouched as he secured one of the stakes to the ground. "Your house needed some cheer."

She stepped over one of the extension cords. "You're going to pay my electric bill," she continued, grumbling as she grabbed one of the other ground stakes and shoved it into the grass to keep the dumb penguins in place.

"I'll pay all your bills." His voice was suddenly very close, and she felt a thrill go up her spine—right before he shoved a cloth over her face and she inhaled something sweet even as she tried to struggle.

That son of a bitch.

CHAPTER 5

—And then there was her.—

This was not how Theo had wanted to start things off with Elliana. Sighing, he glanced over at the woman dozing—okay, unconscious—on the couch next to him.

Suddenly her eyes flew open, and the moment she saw him she sprang into action. Or tried to. She raised her hands, likely to attack him, then saw that her right wrist was handcuffed to his.

He held his palms up. "Listen—"

She screamed and tried to stand, but he held firm, tugging her back down onto the couch, accidentally causing her to splay over him. Yeah, he really hadn't thought through the handcuff thing.

Elliana took a swing at him with her left hand and it would have been a decent shot if she wasn't still woozy.

"Elliana, just stop for a minute." He shifted his head to the side and her fist grazed his ear, landing on the couch behind his head. "Someone wants to kill you!"

She was straddling him now, her knees digging into the cushions, and she had her hands wrapped around his throat as she pinned him against the couch.

And oh god, this position was everything he'd dreamed. Except the choking thing. Or maybe he could get into this? It was kind of hot.

She paused, squeezing harder as she eyed him with rage and murder in her blue eyes. "Are you going to fight back?"

He coughed under the pressure and shook his head. "I don't want to hurt you. I kidnapped you to keep you safe," he rasped out, remaining immobile, even though his instinct was to fight back. But not with her.

Her eyes narrowed even more. "That's the dumbest thing I've ever heard." But her grip eased ever so slightly. Not completely, however. He was counting that as a win.

He dragged in a breath. "Maybe, maybe not."

"Why am I handcuffed to you? And...what the hell! Are we on a boat?!" She glanced around as if seeing her surroundings for the first time. Probably felt the gentle rocking.

"Well, it's a yacht if you want to get technical, since it's a little over forty feet. And I handcuffed you because I thought it would be smart to keep you close when you woke up."

She blinked at him, those blue eyes mesmerizing. "Yeah right," she snorted. "You think you're gonna dump my body out in the ocean? That's actually pretty smart," she growled as she tightened her grip on his neck again, harder this time.

Oh, she was getting her strength back.

He shoved his hands between her arms and snapped out hard against her wrists to dislodge her grip, but she moved fast, tugging him with her to the ground. She shoved her forearm against the front of his throat, and since he didn't want to hurt her, he didn't do what he'd normally do in this situation.

Which was kill her.

Instead he rolled them over and, using his weight and strength against her, he grabbed her free arm and held it above her head as he pinned her in place. It was awkward because his wrist was manacled too.

She bucked against him and his body reacted on instinct, which made her eyes darken.

"You freak!" she screamed.

"Damn it, Elliana! Just listen. I'm sorry!" His stupid dick decided to wake up now? *Come on!* He reached into his pocket and pulled out the key. Showing it to her, he moved slowly as she shot daggers at him with her eyes. Then he unlocked them. As the cuffs fell away, thudding against the plush throw rug, he allowed her to scramble back out from under him.

Aaaand she kicked him in the chest as he started to get up.

He grunted under the blow and rolled back and away from her, keeping his palms out in surrender as he took a step back. "So I probably shouldn't have kidnapped you the way I did."

"No, you shouldn't have kidnapped me at all!" She scanned the interior, definitely looking for a weapon.

Which was why he'd locked up anything he thought she could use before leaving the marina.

"We'll agree to disagree. I'm a hitman and someone put out a hit on you. My dad showed me the contract."

"You *are* trying to kill me!" She grabbed a pillow and threw it at his face.

He batted the blue and white torpedo away, had to block another one as she grabbed the next. "Okay, poor wording. He sent it to me so I could *warn* you. We're all part of a network and this contract just popped up. He knows how I feel about you, so—"

"And how do you feel about me?" she snapped, moving farther away from him back toward the sliding door.

There was no way he was letting her escape—not that there was anywhere to actually go. "Well, I think that's obvious."

Keeping her eye on him, she slowly opened the door, then stepped out onto the back deck. Then she slammed the sliding door behind her.

Sighing, he followed after her, hating the way her shoulders slumped when she saw exactly where they were.

The middle of the ocean with no land or boats or anything else in sight.

"This was the only place I could think of to keep you safe and to explain everything to you where you couldn't run away from me."

Whirling to face him, her jaw tight, she placed her hands on her hips. "Fine, explain. You've got three seconds."

He shoved out a breath. "Like I said, I'm a hitman."

She rolled her eyes.

"Why are you rolling your eyes?" He was being more honest with her than he ever had with anyone. He didn't have the best social skills, or any really, but he didn't go around telling people what he did for a living—she was the first.

She lifted a jerky shoulder and that was when he saw the fear in her eyes. Because of course she was afraid. He had her alone and helpless out here in the middle of the ocean.

He stepped back, putting a little distance between them, then sat at the cushioned outdoor seating area. There was a covering overhead so they had enough shade from the bright sun, but she remained standing, her body tense as she stared him down. The only way to get her to trust him was to be brutally honest.

"My dad keeps tabs on various contracts, and one recently came in—not for us, because you're not our kind of contract," he added. "We have very specific parameters for the kinds of jobs we take on."

She was still silent, watching him, her blue eyes unreadable. But she wasn't attacking him or rolling her eyes, so at least she was listening.

"I might have told him a little about you, and he recognized your name. I considered laying everything out for you at lunch today, but then thought you might think I was crazy and run. I didn't want to risk you putting yourself in danger. So—"

"You were worried I'd think you were crazy, so...you *kidnapped* me instead?" She cocked an eyebrow.

"Yep."

"You don't even sound sorry." The exasperation in her voice mirrored her expression.

"I'm not sorry. You're safe. And now we can figure out who wants to kill you." It was a solid plan. And when he discovered who'd put a hit out on her, they were going to die. Probably slowly, painfully. But they'd be dead by his hand.

"There is no we!" She looked around again, probably for a weapon, then stomped inside without another word.

He found her grabbing a water bottle from the fully stocked refrigerator. He'd asked one of his associates to stock the yacht at the last minute and was impressed by how quickly he'd done it.

Elliana looked at him, then away, then headed even farther away down into one of the staterooms. Either to look for weapons or use the head. Probably both. But he'd cleared out the bathroom of would-be weapons too.

He decided to give her some space and pulled his laptop out of one of the locked cabinets—he'd hidden it because he'd been worried she'd try to knock him out with it and end up destroying it—then pulled up all the files he had to show her.

When she came back up, she still looked pissed, but less afraid than before. And she didn't have any weapons in her hands. So that was something.

He turned his laptop around for her. "All the tabs are right there. Look for yourself." He continued as she sat across from him and started looking at the screen. "Unfortunately, with the way our contracts are set up, it's very difficult to backtrace who put in this request. They're paying with half crypto, and then once the hit is complete, through a numbered bank account only. It's generally how we do things. No names, no identifiers."

She flicked a glance at him, her eyes icy, but didn't respond before she looked back at the screen. She was silent for a while as she scrolled through everything. "You could be making all this up."

"Well, sure. But to what end?"

"I don't know, psychological torture? Because you're a demented freak who gets off on hurting women and dumping their bodies in the ocean? Pick one."

He leaned his head back against the cushioned seating and stared at the glossy wood ceiling. "I don't hurt women," he said quietly. "And I'm sorry for kidnapping you," he finally growled. "I had limited time to make a decision and thought this was the best."

"Fine, then take me home. Or back to shore," she demanded. "If you're so sorry."

"No."

"No?"

"We still don't know who put this hit out on you, or why. And someone took this contract. Someone who is not me!" he added when her eyes turned to flecks of blue ice. "And since I don't know who the actual hitter is, or who put out the contract, this is quite literally the safest place for you. No one knows you're here, and if for some reason someone figures it out, I'll see them coming." Even if someone tried an aerial attack, because he was prepared for that too. But he didn't tell her that in case she got any ideas about his RPG. He didn't want to risk her accidentally blowing up the yacht.

Then they'd really be screwed.

He slid out of the booth and was aware that she was watching him carefully now as he opened one of the cabinets. He pulled out a small bin of decorations and said, "I tried to figure out who would want to kill you, but surprisingly there weren't many people that stood out."

"Why surprisingly? And what are you doing?"

"In my experience, everyone has enemies. But surprisingly only because someone who's partners in such an up-and-coming company should have *more* enemies. Not to mention your military background. But your partners and employees like you, from what I've found. Though to be fair, I've only done surface recon so far." He'd only just found out about the contract, after all.

"Oh my god," she muttered to herself. Then, "Are you putting up Christmas decorations?"

"I felt bad kidnapping you, and my associate—who stocked enough food and water for us for a while—thought it would be nice if I decorated for you."

"Don't bother. I hate Christmas."

"So why is that? Because you got me a Christmas present, so you can't totally hate it, right?" He loved that she'd thought of him enough to buy him specialty coffee. He had a couple presents for her too, but they were at his real home.

She crossed her arms, glowered at him. "I'm not having this conversation."

"Fine, let's talk about who would hate you enough to put a hit out on you. Spurned lover, maybe?" Even the thought of that left the taste of ashes in his mouth.

She snorted.

"So, that's a no?"

"That's a 'none of your fucking business.'"

He lifted a shoulder because he didn't want to talk about her former lovers anyway. "Are you hungry?" he asked as he set up the skinny, small tree at the back of the boat. It was right in front of the sliding glass door that mostly stayed closed.

"No. Maybe." She stood and walked to the refrigerator, peered inside again. "You'll probably poison my food."

He snorted. "If I'd wanted to kill you, I'd have done it earlier when you were unconscious." Or like a dozen times before that when he'd been following her around Miami. He left that part out since she was already so pissed.

She glared at him but didn't refute it as she looked back in the fridge. Instead of food, she pulled out another water and sat back down. "So that house next to mine, it's not really your house, is it?"

"Nope."

"Is it like a murder house?"

"I...I mean, I don't call it that. It's like a cover house, but yes, sometimes I kill people there."

"He says so casually," she muttered to herself. "I can't even be around you right now," she finally snapped, then stood and moved past him and onto the back deck.

"Think about who might want to hurt you," he called out. "We really need to narrow down who the threat might be. Because as soon as I have a name, they're dead."

She slammed the sliding door in response.

CHAPTER 6

— Santa Claus has the right idea: visit people only once a year.—

As Elliana stared out at the dark, rolling waters of the Atlantic—wondering if there were sharks lurking under the surface—she realized that she needed to lull Theo into a false sense of security. Then knock him out. It was the only way she could think to take control of the situation. Because she couldn't take him on one-on-one. When she'd attacked him on the couch, she'd felt his raw strength, had quickly realized when he'd flipped them that he'd been holding back.

Once she got free, she had to figure out who the hell wanted to kill her.

Because she wasn't so sure he was lying about that. He could be, of course, but she couldn't figure out to what end. And all the info he'd shown her had looked so damn real.

"Beautiful, isn't it?" he asked in that deep rumble.

She'd been aware of him stepping out onto the rear deck as she stared at the sun fading into the ocean. "What?"

"The sunset. Also your ass."

Blinking, she glanced up at him and found him looking down at her with that cheeky grin. And those dumb, adorable dimples.

Dimples! On a hitman! It was just all sorts of wrong. And he wasn't wearing a shirt again.

"Why are you naked?" Okay, he wasn't actually naked, but whatever. Semantics.

Now he was the one to blink before he patted his flat, ripped stomach. "I'm wearing pants, not naked."

Oh god, was she drooling? She looked back at the sunset, could actually appreciate the oranges, pinks and purples streaking the sky as darkness started to take over. But okay, she was struggling to focus when a built god was standing right next to her.

"I spilled some oil on my shirt when I was cooking. I wanted to let you know I made dinner, if you're hungry."

She bit back a smartass retort. She needed to make him think she was starting to be okay with all this, to get him to let his guard down. Being rude and grumpy wouldn't get her what she needed. "Thanks, I am kind of hungry."

His expression softened as he stepped back and headed inside—though he didn't fully give her his back, she noted. His broad, muscular back she'd fantasized more than once about sinking her fingers into while he rode her. But that was before he'd knocked her out and kidnapped her and trapped her on this boat.

Or yacht. Whatever.

As she stepped inside, she inhaled the scent of something delicious, but she was momentarily distracted by the tree. "What happened to your Christmas tree?" The little pink flamingos were all askew, half the lights were out and there were a couple gobs of tinsel that looked as if they'd been thrown on.

"What's wrong with it?" His voice was distracted as he moved up next to her, and she realized he was watching her.

She narrowed her gaze at him. "Did you do it like this so it would drive me crazy?"

He blinked, the confusion on his face real. Or at least she believed it. "What are you talking about?"

Grumbling to herself, while cursing her mild OCD tendencies, she started with the tinsel. Which she more or less hated, but if it was spread out correctly, it would make the tree glitter. Not that she should care. And she didn't. But if she was going to be stuck looking at a Christmas tree, it was damn well going to look good. "If you're going to do something, you can't half-ass it. If you do, you end up with this." She held up her right thumb, showing off that she was missing the tip. "This is because once upon a time, I was a dumbass who didn't double check something."

She was startled when he lightly grasped her wrist, kissed her messed-up thumb right on the tip. She wasn't sensitive about her thumb, but the sensation of his lips on her took her off guard, totally threw her world off-kilter even more than the whole kidnapping thing.

Yanking her hand away, she gave him her back as she tried to quell that punch of adrenaline from his light touch.

She thought he'd move away but instead she realized he was *smelling* her hair. She elbowed him in the ribs, gently. "Back up, weirdo. You can't go around smelling random women."

"You're not random, and you're the only woman I want to smell."

"Such a strange conversation," she muttered as she moved on to straightening the little flamingo and palm tree ornaments. They were all different, she realized, and delicate. And okay, really, really adorable. Not that she'd ever tell him that. But each flamingo was doing something silly—one had a sign that said *Merry Flockin' Christmas,* another was ice skating while drinking a martini, and yet another had a gnome riding on its back. Which was weird because she would expect an elf.

But maybe gnomes liked Christmas too.

When she heard him move away, she glanced behind her and saw that he'd retreated to the kitchen and was plating what was definitely spaghetti.

She wasn't sure why, but she missed having him so close to her. Which made no sense.

"I have red and white wine," he called out, and she suddenly clued in that she was staring at his ass.

Oh, no. Noooo. "Ah, white please." Because she was going to drink with him, eat with him, hang out with him. And as soon as he went to sleep, she was going to make her move. Because once again life had proven that she couldn't trust anyone who hadn't proven themselves to her. Especially not hot men.

She wasn't totally sure how she was going to escape yet, but she was getting the hell out of here one way or another. "So, what happens if we can't figure out who wants me dead?" she asked, giving the now organized-looking tree a happy nod as she stepped back. There, that looked proper. Not that she cared. Nope.

"We'll set a trap and lure out the hitter. From there, it'll go one of two ways." He paused. "Or three ways. One, I'll be able to convince the hitter who took the contract to back off—which is unlikely—or two, I'll kill him. After he's dead, the contract will reactivate. I'll grab it, and from there we'll figure out who put it out in the first place. Not that we'll stop working that angle during the first bit, but if it comes to that, it'll give us some breathing room until we figure out who wants you dead. Or three, after I kill the hitter, I pretend to be him and bait whoever hired him."

Frowning, she sat on one of the cream-colored cushions in the kitchen area...or maybe it was called a galley. She didn't know much about boats, but it was clear this was a *very* expensive one. The interior had all top-of-the-line appliances that blended seamlessly into everything else. And it didn't have the salty, musty smell she associated with boats. This one smelled like money.

"You're very confident you'll be able to kill whoever is after me." Not that she'd admit it out loud, but she liked that he genuinely seemed concerned for her safety—even if he was planning to kill someone.

He placed a stemless glass in front of her, filled it with an expensive brand of pinot grigio she recognized. "Would you rather I was worried? Because that bastard doesn't stand a chance, whoever he is."

"You think it's a man."

"Likelihood is higher, but I never rule anything out." He set a steaming plate in front of her before he poured his own glass and got his own food.

Even though he was her kidnapper, she still waited until he sat to touch her food—because of her plan. She was luring him into a sense of false security.

"Considering you work in a male-dominated industry and you're a billionaire, the chances of a man wanting to kill you are definitely higher."

She snorted at the word billionaire.

He lifted an eyebrow as he began twirling his noodles onto his fork. "Why is that funny?"

"I don't know, I guess technically I am." But it felt weird to say or even think it. Weston had his shit together, had started investing almost immediately after they went public and everything had exploded. Her lifestyle was pretty much the same as it had been before.

She wished she could just shove her money under her mattress and pretend it didn't exist. Not that she didn't like money, or rather the buffer it gave her. The safety net. Something she'd never had growing up. Not even close.

But that kind of wealth also made her profoundly uncomfortable. And a possible target, along with anyone she cared about. The only big change she'd made was that she'd donated a lot of it to various charities.

"There's no technical about it."

She bit her bottom lip. "You think someone wants me dead because I'm rich?"

"Not specifically, no. But I'm playing the odds that money ties into this somehow. Because people are usually predictable. And there isn't a contract out on either of your business partners, so in the end I think this will have to do with money and be personal." He shrugged, but she didn't miss the flash of rage in his eyes.

Oh, he really was pissed about the contract.

It shouldn't make her feel all warm and fuzzy inside, but she liked that he cared about her. *Wait, no! No, no, no.* She took a sip of her wine, shoved all those thoughts down. She wasn't going to go all Stockholm syndrome with him. Absolutely not.

"Could it be someone in your family?" His question was casual enough, but there was something in his tone that was off.

She set her fork down. She was estranged from all of them after the way they'd betrayed her. "My family doesn't have enough money to put out a contract like the one you showed me."

"Okay, that's not a no." Now he was really frowning.

"I don't...I mean, I don't think anyone in my family would do this. It wouldn't make sense for them to want me dead," she said, not bothering to hide her bitterness. Even if she was estranged from her family, she'd still paid off her father's mortgage and bought him a new vehicle because he'd needed it. But she sure as hell didn't talk to him or her stepmom—and definitely not to her stepsister.

Theo simply raised his eyebrows.

She ignored the question in his gaze, turned back to her food. "This is pretty good."

"Pretty good? I'll have to up my game next time." That genial note was back in his voice, but she wasn't fooled, could still see the curiosity in his pale tiger eyes. The predator lurking in the shadows behind the beautiful amber. He might smile easily, but this man was a sneaky...tiger. That's what he was. A big, sneaky tiger in human skin.

"What's that look?" His voice was a low rumble, Mr. Sexy back in full force. "Because you look as if you've just figured something out."

"I have no look." She certainly wasn't going to tell him that she was thinking of him as a sneaky tiger in her head. That was weird, even for her. "I'm just enjoying my dinner with my very polite kidnapper." She couldn't help but needle him, was perversely happy to see the flare of annoyance in his eyes. Oh, he didn't like being reminded he was a kidnapper?

Well, she didn't like being kidnapped.

"So, you seem to know a whole lot about me, but I don't know much about you." She took another bite, watched him expectantly.

"What do you want to know?" He leaned back, his huge frame taking up all the space on his side of the built-in booth area.

"Everything."

"That covers a lot."

He watched her for a long moment and yep, she saw that sneakiness in his eyes as he calculated something. "I'll play you cards for information."

"Cards?" She twirled another bunch of noodles and sauce.

"Poker or whatever you choose. If you win a hand, I answer your question."

"I like the sound of that." She wasn't great at poker, but she slayed at blackjack. "Wait, what happens if I lose?"

"You have to take off an article of clothing."

She blinked. "Seriously? Like strip poker or strip Uno or whatever?"

"Yep." The edges of his mouth curved up just a fraction.

"Oh my god, I thought you had more depth than that. Apparently all men are predictable."

He grinned, showing off dimples that she tried to ignore. Unfortunately she was a mere mortal and he was so damn adorable. And murdery. Couldn't forget that.

But he was such an adorable killer. *Gah!*

"Yep. I'm a simple man who wants to see you naked. Which is only fair, considering you've seen all of me. Many times." His voice dropped low again and she felt that drop straight to her core.

Heat flooded between her legs at whatever that look was he was giving her. It was almost challenging, as if he just knew she was going to say no.

So of course she took the challenge. "Sounds good to me. If you've got cards, I'll shuffle."

***

"You tricked me," Elliana grumbled as she took off her shirt, threw it at Theo's face.

He snort-laughed as he batted away the shirt and she wondered how much wine he'd had. Then she looked at her own almost empty glass, realized she should probably stop drinking too.

"You picked the game, so how did I trick you?"

"I've learned nothing useful about you other than you have parents, a sister, and you've won all but two rounds." He'd taken off his socks as a sort of concession because he kept winning, but it was more obnoxious than anything. She wanted answers to her questions, not to see his feet. Okay, maybe she wanted to see them a little. But him answering two of her questions was nothing in the scheme of things. "And I've already seen you naked anyway." She tried to sound dismissive, but he wasn't buying it, if that intense look was any indication.

She glanced down, saw that her nipples were showing through her lacy lavender bra. *Oops.* "This reaction is because I'm cold," she muttered, grabbing a blue pillow with little white anchors all over it and holding it in her lap to cover herself. Well, it was mostly because she was cold.

"Uh huh." His grin was pure mischievousness as he said, "Stay."

She flipped over her next card, saw that her cards added up to nineteen, one less than his amount, and groaned again. "I don't know how, but you're cheating."

"I didn't take you for a sore loser." He leaned back, not bothering to hide the fact that he was staring.

"Fine." She knew she could just refuse to keep going, but that wasn't how she was wired. She'd agreed to play this dumb game, so she reached behind her back and unhooked her bra...and loved the way his eyes went molten as she slowly removed the far-too-expensive piece of lingerie—one of her few splurges that were just for her. After years of living in the sandbox, of not being able to take showers in private or sometimes at all, she wanted soft, silky material against her skin whenever possible. As she tossed her bra away, she grinned and kept the pillow against her chest.

"Hey, who's cheating now?" he demanded.

"You never said I couldn't hide myself with a pillow."

"It messes with the spirit of the game."

"Well, I'm going to pull the kidnapping card one more time and say that I get special treatment because you *kidnapped* me."

He grumbled, almost pouting, but shrugged. "I take off my clothes for you all the time," he said, starting to shuffle the cards.

Expertly, she thought. So, so expertly. Clearly he was a man of many secrets.

"First, I never asked you to... So why did you start doing that, anyway?" The first time he'd slowly taken his clothes off for her, she'd been too shocked to look away. The second time... *Whew*, he'd done more than take off his clothes. And she'd become addicted to watching him.

His grin was back as he continued mixing the cards. "Because I liked the way you watched me. At first I thought you might want to kill me. But when I realized that you were just a very sexy pervert, I decided to give you a show."

Despite everything, she snickered. "It *is* pretty weird that I just started spying on you." She'd never spied on anyone before until him.

"Why did you?"

"Uh-uh. No way, I'm not telling you anything else. You already know too much." She hiccupped, then cursed.

Which made him laugh, a real one that sent so many ribbons of heat to her core. "You even hiccup cute," he said, still laughing as he dealt cards.

She hated that more warmth spread through her, that her awareness of him seemed to be growing, getting worse. She wanted to crawl into his lap, straddle him, and find out exactly how good he felt sliding inside her. She was supposed to be luring him into a false sense of security, and okay, she was doing a pretty good job of it. But she was also forgetting that she needed him to go to sleep so she could take over the boat. Not that she knew how to drive it, but she understood how to work GPS systems, and the radio system was simple enough. She'd figure it out.

As she picked up her cards, a shiver racked her as she fought off another chill.

"You're freezing," Theo said suddenly, frowning at her, all concerned, and oh god, his mouth was perfect.

She stared at his bottom lip, imagined nibbling on it, then realized he was saying something else. "What?"

He just shook his head, then grabbed a throw from the main seating area behind the galley. When he leaned in close to wrap it around her, she found herself inhaling his scent much the same way he'd done to her. Oh yeah, she'd definitely had too much wine.

"You should have said something," he murmured, gathering up all the cards.

"Hey, we're done?"

"You're definitely done. You're clearly exhausted."

She didn't argue as he started cleaning up their plates, which they'd abandoned earlier. Instead, she took one last sip of her wine and made her way to the long, cushy couch and lay down.

"The bedroom is yours," he called out as he washed the dishes.

She ignored him as she tucked the blanket up to her neck. She was just going to close her eyes for a couple minutes.

Then once he went to sleep, it was on.

Chapter 7

—The best things in life are weird and unpredictable.—

Elliana glanced around the cabin, her heart racing. She'd fallen asleep for a lot longer than she'd planned. She'd just meant to close her eyes.

Stupid, delicious wine.

As she eased the two blankets off her, she realized Theo must have added another one when he'd apparently tucked her in as tight as a burrito. And he must have added another pillow under her head too.

She saw a neatly folded pile of clothes next to the couch and slid the light sweater and jeans on, not bothering with a bra. It was still dark outside but there was enough dim blue lighting built in along the interior panels that she had a decent enough view of things.

Staying as quiet as possible, she hurried through the cabin and galley to the two cushy seats where the cockpit was. The dashboard was fairly complex, but she had more than enough experience hacking. Of course, she normally had her tools with her, but she got to work, trying to pull up the GPS.

Unfortunately, the screen was completely locked. And without her tools, she couldn't begin to crack the login code. Unless she managed to reset the entire panel, but that could backfire on her.

Damn it!

Okay, new plan.

Next, she tried the various cabinets above the sink and countertop, found all of them locked, including the one where he'd tucked the laptop away.

She wasn't going to let a little lock stop her.

After quietly rummaging around in the drawers, she found some random cutlery and managed to pry open the top cabinet, only bending the lock a little and with no sound. She was currently stealth personified. No laptop though, so he must have moved it once she'd gone to sleep.

Of course he had.

Her gaze strayed to the little hallway that would lead to the bedroom, and her heart rate kicked up. If she could get that laptop, she'd just reset the damn thing and make contact with Weston and Van and tell them what was going on. She should be able to figure out her coordinates once she reset it as well.

Decision made, she moved quietly down the small set of stairs that led to the primary cabin toward the bow. She'd used the head earlier, but hadn't found much she could use as a weapon. She had, however, found a few supplies she could use to make an explosive.

But she wasn't going to risk that, not out here in the middle of the ocean. That was her option only in an emergency situation where she had no choice.

She slipped through the half-open doorway without making a sound, grateful for all her military training. She might like to blow shit up, but she knew how to be a ghost when necessary.

The bedroom was dim, with a thin blue light running the length of the room. And there was a beam of pale blue light coming from the attached bathroom. The bed itself was swathed in too many shadows so all she could make out was a big lump of darkness in the middle of it. At least she could hear Theo breathing, so she knew he was in here. And he was breathing that steady rhythm of someone in a deep sleep.

But it was way too quiet in here. *Damn it.* She couldn't start moving around blindly, trying to open cabinets. He'd definitely wake up. He was a freaking hitman. Of course he'd be a light sleeper. She'd have to try in the morning when he was otherwise occupied.

"I hope you're here to join me." A little lamp clicked on.

She resisted the urge to jump, proud of herself for the control. "You're delusional." So much for lulling him into a false sense of security. That ship had sailed. Literally and figuratively.

Propped up on a couple pillows, he slid his hands behind his head and watched her with raw lust. He wasn't even trying to hide it. The covers were pooled at his waist as he watched with those tiger eyes. And of course he didn't have a shirt on, so his naked torso was on display, all his muscles begging for her to touch. To kiss. Maybe bite a little.

"I'm not delusional about how much you want me," he murmured, watching her with a growing hunger.

She made a scoffing sound, but that was all she could muster up. Considering she'd been watching him for months, yeah, *clearly* she wanted him. Even now in spite of this messed-up situation. "You put a lock on the driving mechanism. What happens to me if you, like...have a heart attack or something? I'll just be stuck out here alone without being able to call for help."

"If I don't check in with one of my associates, they'll be by here to check on you, so that alleviates that problem. They have strict instructions to keep you safe at all costs."

She gritted her teeth, even as she felt a little better. If he keeled over, at least she wasn't going to be stuck out here forever. "What if a storm rolls in—"

"I'm keeping an eye on the weather and we're not that far from land. Too far to swim though." He was still watching her like a predator watched prey. But not in a creepy way that made her want to hide. Nope, in the way that made her want to take off all her clothes.

And sweet lord, she liked it. There was definitely something wrong with her.

"I have a proposal," he said when she didn't respond.

Elliana narrowed her gaze. "What?"

"You let me make you come."

She blinked, taken off guard by his boldness. "I'm not having sex with you!"

"I mean orally. I want to go down on you. I've been dreaming about making you come against my tongue for months."

The way he watched her with that hooded gaze, biting his bottom lip, told her that he really had been fantasizing about that. And damn, that was hot.

"You set the rhythm," he continued. "You get all the orgasms you want. It's a win-win."

"In exchange for what?"

"Nothing. I just want to bring you pleasure."

She didn't believe him. There were always strings attached to everything. "And if I say no?" Why was she even entertaining this? His "proposal" was bonkers. It wasn't happening. *Nope.*

"Then you say no and nothing happens."

Glaring at him, she spun on her heel and headed back up to the main cabin. She was glad when he didn't follow her. Feeling out of sorts, she stretched out on the couch and tried not to obsess over his words. He was just messing with her, right?

Ugh. She knew he wasn't, because she'd seen the heat in his eyes, damn him.

And now he was under her skin. Well, more under than he already was. Because all she could think about was taking him up on his offer, riding his face until she came and...

She punched one of the pillows and turned over, trying to get comfortable, even as she knew that at this point it was an impossibility.

Not after he'd just lobbed that metaphorical bomb at her and all she wanted to do was take him up on his delicious offer. To just let go of all her worries for a bit.

***

Elliana rolled over again, glared up at the glossy wood-paneled ceiling. Then she looked over at the wall clock in the dimness. Only an hour had passed, though it felt like a hell of a lot longer.

She kept replaying Theo's words over and over, particularly when he'd said, *I've been dreaming about making you come against my tongue for months.*

Because she was pretty certain those were the hottest words ever spoken in the English language.

Every time she thought about what he'd said, her skin flushed hot. So basically she'd been lying here turned on for the last hour because it was *all* she'd been able to think about.

Annoyed with herself, with *him* for getting into her head, with the whole damn world, she shoved her blanket off and headed back down to the bedroom cabin and found Theo reading with the little lamp on next to him.

He set his book down, his gaze raking over her.

"So you're just down here reading?" she demanded, then felt foolish, but she'd been up there crawling out of her skin and needed him to do something about it. Because she'd decided she was going to take him up on his offer.

She was already hot, hungry for him, the need to ease that ache between her legs so great she could barely think straight. Maybe that had been his plan. And if so, it had worked.

"Nope. I was pretending to be casual but I've tried to read the same page a dozen times. I wanted to follow after you but I didn't because of the power imbalance between us. I shouldn't have said what I said."

Wait, what? Oh, no. No, no, no.

"You shouldn't have said you wanted to make me come?" She was at the foot of the bed now, her decision already made. He couldn't back out now!

"Oh, I still mean it," he rasped out. "I really want to, but I did technically kidnap you, so—"

"There's no technically about it."

He rolled his eyes, shrugged in that sexy, annoying way of his. "Fine. I 'relocated you'—temporarily, I might add—while I try to hunt down who wants you dead. But until then, I won't ask to give you orgasms again." He paused, then added, "Even if I really, really want to." His eyes were practically glowing now.

So he dangled a carrot in front of her and then thought he could take it away? *Oh, hell no.* She didn't think he was trying to play games, but if he was, she was going to win.

With orgasms. Lots of them.

She tugged her sweater over her head, then shimmied out of her jeans before she crawled into bed next to him, stretching out slowly, arching her back and enjoying the way he watched her, the sudden leap of hunger in his eyes.

"The bed's mine now," she practically purred. "And for the record, I'm on birth control." She just thought that was something he might want to know.

He stared, his eyes sweeping over her breasts, down to her skimpy panties, all the way down to her toes, then back up again. Then he repeated it, as if he couldn't drink his fill.

Her nipples hardened as he watched her as if he could eat her up. She knew what was below his pants, had seen him stroke himself off and felt the outline of his erection before, and now all she wanted was to feel him thrusting inside her.

He cleared his throat as his eyes met hers again. "You want me to go to the upper cabin?" he rasped out.

"I want you to do what you promised."

He stared at her, his amber eyes slightly narrowed, and she was pretty sure he was torn on what to do.

So she reached down and started to slide her panties off. She knew she was putting a lot of trust in a man who'd handcuffed her and kidnapped her. But right now she was going to rely on her instinct—the one that had helped make her successful and saved her from getting blown up multiple times in war zones—and get some promised orgasms. She just needed to take the edge off so she could think clearly again. That was all.

You're crazy if that's what you think, the little voice in her head whispered. So she ignored it.

He moved quicker than she'd have thought possible, given his size, with an agility that was impressive as he rolled over and knelt between her splayed legs. He placed his hands on hers where she held the waistband of her panties and took over, pulling the scrap of material the rest of the way down her legs. "This is my job." His tone was intense and serious.

The way he got all growly sent a shiver of hunger rolling through her, and on instinct she closed her legs, trying to ease that growing ache. Now that she was close to him, lying on the sheets he'd been sleeping on, smelling him, her senses were going into overdrive.

He still had on jogging pants but his erection was very visible. And something told her he'd only kept pants on because of her—because he *had* to be the kind of man who slept naked.

"We stop when you say stop," he said as he crawled up her body, caging her in. Overwhelming her with his size and power—but in the best way possible. "I'm not going to take advantage of you. This is only about your pleasure right now." He was hovering right above her, his amber eyes on her mouth, his hunger a bright, burning star.

"I wouldn't let you take advantage of me," she whispered, sliding her hands up his chest, savoring the feel of all his strength under her fingertips. Good god, this man was built everywhere. Seeing him and touching him were two very different things. And if he didn't put out the fire he'd started, she would kill him. "If anything, I'm taking advantage of you."

"How?" he murmured as he leaned closer, his mouth an inch from hers, his warm breath feathering over her skin, sending shivers of delight rolling through her.

"I'm using you so you let your guard down, and then I'll use that to my advantage to escape," she breathed out. "Maybe I'll tie you up."

He nipped her bottom lip. "You're not supposed to tell me your plan." Then he nipped her again.

And she felt that playful little nip right to her core. As if he'd actually touched her between her legs. Heat pooled low in her belly and she resisted the urge to wrap her entire body around him and hump him like a horny teenager. "I believe in honesty."

"I can give you honesty," he growled as he slanted his mouth over hers.

She opened for him, all of her wanting to believe that he would be real with her. And it was as if something invisible between them snapped free.

His big body came down on hers, but he wasn't too heavy. If anything, she liked the pressure, and loved the feel of his thick erection pressing against her core.

"If you decide to tie me up," he murmured against her mouth, "feel free to do dirty things to my body. As much as you want. I consent to all of it."

Despite everything, she laughed. And damn, it felt so good to let go. This whole situation was completely messed up, but she found that with this weirdo she could be her weird self too.

And it was freeing in a way she'd never experienced.

"For the record," he continued, "I'm clean. Haven't been with anyone since before you started spying on me."

Oh, hell. She hadn't been with anyone in longer than that, but she loved that he'd been celibate during that time.

He grinned against her mouth before he began nibbling along her jaw, taking his time as he whispered, "Every time you watched me naked, I thought of you as I jacked off. Imagined what you'd taste like."

His words were like gasoline to the fire burning inside her. "Stop talking," was about all she could manage as he cupped her breasts, slowly rubbed his thumbs over her hard nipples.

He was teasing her with an ease that said he had all the time in the world. And when he bent his head to one of her breasts, he let out the most incredible sound of appreciation.

"From the moment I saw you," he murmured before he nipped one nipple, flicked his tongue over it in tight little circles, "even when I thought you were out to kill me, I wanted you so badly I couldn't think straight."

His words sent off another wave of heat inside her. At this point, she was going to combust even before she came. Hell, maybe she'd just climax from his words alone. She slid her hands over his shoulders and biceps, memorizing the feel of them, the way his muscles flexed under her touch. She wanted to pull him closer, but she also didn't want him to stop what he was doing. So she just gripped him tight, dug her fingernails into his taut skin and held on.

As he moved to her other breast, sucking on her nipple hard, she inhaled sharply. Then she spread her thighs and angled her hips so that she was rubbing her core against his still-covered erection.

She groaned as he moved against her, felt the actual size of him. She'd known he was big, but again, seeing it and feeling it were two very different things.

Her inner walls clenched as she imagined being filled by him. Stretched and pleasured.

"Can I touch you here?" he asked as he gently cupped her mound. "Inside you?"

"Yes." She barely got the word out, her throat so tight, all her muscles bunched in anticipation.

"You're not going to regret this?" He paused, looked up at her, and she could see the seriousness in his eyes. As if he really cared.

Oh, she was so gone for this guy, kidnapper/killer or not. "No regrets." No way was she regretting this. Once upon a time she'd played things safe, but those days were long behind her. "What about you?" she asked suddenly when he went to dip his head to her other breast.

"I could never regret you." Five blunt words as he slid a thick finger inside her slick folds.

Oooohhh. She rolled her hips against his hand, almost embarrassed by how wet she was. Almost but not quite, considering his massive erection.

They both wanted each other with a frightening need that, okay, unsettled her. This man was a straight-up killer, but every instinct she possessed told her that he'd burn the world down around them to keep her safe. She had no defense against that. It was as if he simply stripped her bare with his need for her.

"You're so wet," he groaned even as he moved off her.

Before she could protest, try to tug him back onto her, his big, callused hands pressed her thighs open as he crouched between them.

The little lamp gave off more than enough light so that she could see every single thing. And the way he inhaled, as if he'd die without tasting her... She was about to come from that alone.

Reflexively, her walls tightened around his finger, making him grin that predator grin. She tightened them again, this time intentionally.

With his gaze on hers, he slid a second finger inside her as he dipped his head between her legs and, with no preamble, sucked on her clit.

"Theo!" Her entire body jolted from the sensation of him kissing her so intimately.

"Say my name again," he demanded, the reverberation of his words sending even more pleasure curling through her.

She slid her fingers through his dark hair. "I wasn't sure if it was really your name." The words were out before she could stop herself, but they were true. She had been wondering, and trust didn't come easy to her.

He growled again, but this time she couldn't understand what he said against her clit. And she didn't really care as he began stroking his fingers in and out of her in a soft, gentle rhythm.

"I'm going to come," she blurted, more from surprise than anything else. It was like these last months had been building to this. Or maybe that was just in her mind, but she didn't care because her ridiculously hot neighbor had his mouth between her legs, making her feel things she had never felt before.

Her hips jerked again when he curved his fingers inside her with each stroke, and her orgasm punched through her in wave after wave, taking over everything.

For a moment she saw stars as she fell back against the fluffy bedding, and then he was on top of her, looking very satisfied with himself as he stared down at her. "One down, many more to go," he said, still grinning as he brushed his mouth over hers. "Or come."

"I'm gonna need a minute," she rasped out. Or a couple. But she reached for the top of his pants, started to push them down. Because she wanted to make him feel as good as he'd made her. And something told her that they were just getting started.

"I don't want you to feel—"

"I swear to god if you say something stupid like you don't want me to feel pressured or something along those lines, I won't be stroking your gorgeous cock. I might punch it." She'd been fantasizing about touching him, making him come, for months. And she also wanted him inside her for her next orgasm. So it was a little selfish.

That got a grin out of him. "Is it weird that I like when you're violent?" he asked, even as he shoved his pants down, managed to kick them off without much effort.

"I think we're past the point of wondering if any of this is weird." And she didn't care at all. "Now lie back."

As they switched places, she enjoyed the view of Theo beneath her, realized she'd need hours and hours to drink her fill of him. She wanted to kiss and touch him everywhere.

Still feeling a little weak from her climax, she wrapped her fingers around his thick erection as she straddled his upper thighs. The pose put her in a unique position, limiting his movement, and she liked being in control.

Keeping her gaze on him, she stroked him once, softly, and watched his expression as she did.

He gritted his teeth, digging his fingers into the sheets. "Harder."

He was so gorgeous it almost hurt to look at him. "Like this?" she whispered, only increasing the pressure a fraction.

He let out a long groan. "It doesn't matter. Your hands are on me. I'm going to embarrass myself sooner or later anyway," he admitted.

Something about the raw honesty of his words hit her right in the chest. She gripped his length and began stroking harder, watching the way his head rolled back, savoring the sound of ecstasy he made as she rubbed her thumb over his slick crown.

Before she could change her mind, she slightly shifted her position and scooted between his legs instead of caging him in. Then she went down on him, taking that thick length into her mouth as his hips jerked off the bed.

"Fuck!" The word was a guttural sound torn from his throat. "Elliana, baby. I...I'm close. Move if you don't want me to come in your mouth."

The sweet way he called her baby? Oh, she was definitely screwed. She sucked him deeper and true to his word, he completely let go.

Apparently both of them had been right on the edge, ready to combust, because that was exactly what he did, losing control as he came hard.

She might be in a position of control now, but the truth was, she was completely unraveled inside. He'd stripped her bare, right down to her soul, and she didn't think she'd recover if this man broke her heart. If he lied to her.

Breathing unsteadily, she climbed up his body, collapsing on his chest and loving the way he held her close. Normally she wasn't a cuddler, but right now she'd make an exception for this complicated man.

"The code to the driving panel is your birthday," he murmured. "Year included."

Still in a bit of a haze, she looked up at him as his words, the actual meaning, registered. "Seriously?" Her birthday? She swallowed hard, unable to say anything at all.

His expression was hard to read as he watched her. "I won't stop you if you want to leave. But fair warning, I *will* follow you."

Shaking her head, she lay back against his chest. She wasn't going anywhere. Not right now anyway. Maybe...ever.

She quickly shut down that little thought that had popped in her head with such sudden force, she couldn't unthink it. She was in so over her head with this man.

Chapter 8

—It's amazing how one day someone walks into your life, and then the next day you wonder how you lived without them.—

Elliana stretched out in bed as beams of sunlight warmed her face. She cracked open her eyes as Theo stepped down into the cabin, carrying two mugs of what had to be coffee.

"You're awake." He seemed positively pleased by that idea.

Which made her smile, warmth spreading through her chest at the way he looked at her. Even if he was really cheery for how early it was. Groaning, she rolled over and pulled the covers over her head. "Too sunny!" He should learn now that she could be cranky in the mornings.

A moment later, the covers were tugged off her and she fought off a chill as the cooler air rushed over her naked body. Ugh, fine, she'd get up. In a minute.

Probably. Hmm, maybe Theo could convince her to wake up with his—

"Who did that to you?" His voice was blade sharp, his tone pure ice.

Alarmed by the abrupt change, Elliana rolled over and opened her eyes to watch him set the mugs down then crawl onto the bed.

"What?" She had no idea what he was talking about, but he looked pissed.

"This." Reaching around her, he rubbed his fingers over her long-healed scar on the right side of her back. His touch was light, gentle. "Who. Did. *This*."

She liked his hands on her, but didn't want to talk about what had happened. "Why does it matter?"

"Because their days are numbered." There he went, all murdery again.

And there she went, liking his protective tone far too much. "It's from shrapnel, so stop sharpening all those imaginary knives. Or whatever you're thinking of right now. No one did this to me. Well...not me specifically. I was simply collateral damage."

Theo still had that dark look and she preferred her hitman to have a big smile, so she took his face between her hands and kissed him.

"It was a long time ago and I'm fine." But not everyone she'd been with that day had survived. And now, of all times, she didn't want to dwell on their loss. Not when she still had those images etched into her memory, the pain stamped into her heart. She was lucky all she'd walked away with was a scar. "Now where's my coffee?"

"I don't like this at all." He was still scowling, but he picked up the coffee and handed it to her.

It felt weird to be so comfortable and intimate with him. And lounging in bed and drinking coffee felt like a very "couple-y" thing to do. At that thought, a bit of panic slid through her veins. Things were moving way too fast between them and she didn't know nearly enough about him. Other than what he looked and sounded like when he came. So there was that.

"Is the code for the driving panel really my birthday?" she asked, instead of giving in to the urge to pepper him with questions.

"Yep. And I left my phone, your phone, and my computer out in the galley. You can use all of them anytime you want." Then he gave her the unlock code to his phone and computer.

She snuggled up next to him, still holding her mug as she leaned on him, enjoying his warmth and strength. "I've been wanting to ask you questions but I thought you might lie to me. Now I don't think you will...soooo, can I ask questions?" *Yep. No control at all.*

"You can ask anything you want." He kissed the top of her head, turned more so that he entangled his big, long legs with hers. "But I want to know what happened to your thumb."

"I'm going to spill my coffee if you keep this up," she murmured.

He just grunted as if he didn't care.

So she continued when he simply bent down and kissed her thumb while she was holding her mug. "Ah, like I said before. I was distracted and screwed up. We'd just lost..." She cleared her throat, not wanting to relive any of those days. "I'd lost people close to me and we had an upcoming mission. One that involved explosives—I miscalculated and my poor thumb paid the price." She'd never made that mistake again.

Silently, he kissed her thumb again, then tightened his grip around her all protectively.

She wasn't sure she did either. "So, I want details about who you are, how you ended up as a hitman. Because that's not a typical job." One didn't fill out a job application and presto, hired hitman.

He was quiet, his big body tensing against hers. She understood she was asking for honesty, but she'd made herself about as vulnerable as possible, was still trusting him, even after he'd kidnapped her. Whether it was for her own good or not wasn't even the point.

After what they'd shared, she needed him to trust her, to be real with her. To have faith that she wouldn't betray him. It mattered so much that if he didn't open up to her...

She didn't want to think about it even as disappointment started that cascade inside her.

"My sister was hurt," he finally said. He cleared his throat as if he was trying to clear away shards of glass. "Raped. I just hate saying the word," he continued, his voice tight, the words clipped. "But I need to because that's what it was. And her rapist wasn't convicted, was found not guilty." In that moment, the violence rolling off him was palpable, so clear she could almost see it in the air.

This was something she actually understood, had felt herself before. Helpless and full of rage at an injustice she couldn't change.

"It happened when she was a freshman in college. He was a rich prick with connections, his father on the board of trustees, their lineage dating back to the Mayflower or some bullshit. It's a tale as old as time." His words were laced with rage. "Then the bastard decided to terrorize her more when he found out she was pregnant by demanding shared custody. She would have been forced to see him for years."

Elliana realized he was balling up the sheets beneath him with his free hand, his knuckles turning white. So she set her coffee down and leaned more into him, wrapping her arm all the way around him as she lay her head on his chest.

"I—and my parents—wanted to take care of him immediately. Even before the original criminal trial. But my sister has too big of a heart and wanted to protect her child and let the justice system do what it was supposed to. She demanded we do nothing." He snorted in disgust. "So we all sat back and did just that. Nothing. She'd already had control taken away from her. I couldn't do it to her again, even in a different sort of way."

His heart rate was slightly elevated, but he took a deep breath. "When I think about how I waited, I get so damn angry at myself. When it was clear that she was going to have to drop thousands on a lawyer and be dragged through a custody battle after the baby was born, I did what I had to do. Especially since the judge was corrupt as hell, had a buried connection to the guy's father. I knew what was going to happen, and I simply couldn't sit back and wait for her to take on even more pain when the judge ordered her to share custody of her baby with her rapist."

"He was the first person you killed?"

"Yep. But not the last. And I'm not sorry. Not one single part of me is sorry for what I did. I made sure she had an airtight alibi, had witnesses, wasn't even in the same state when it happened. I'd do it again and again, in this lifetime or another one." There was no hiding the savagery in his voice.

"Good."

He jolted slightly against her, so she looked up at him, found him watching her with curiosity. "You're not disgusted?"

"Nope. How's your sister now?"

"Amazing." His face changed completely. "Perfect, even. Her daughter doesn't know anything about her biological father and never will. My parents paid a visit to the dead asshole's parents' summer house, burned it down to the studs, then made it clear that if they contacted my sister again, next time it would be their main home with them in it.

"I'm pretty sure my mom did more than that, because there's never once been a hint of them trying to come after us or attempting to meet their granddaughter. They knew or at least suspected one of us killed their son, but their sense of self-preservation is higher than any love—if they ever had any—for their dead son. But to answer your question, my sister is the best. Although she claims that my niece is a handful and I spoil her too much." He grinned, looking completely unrepentant.

Glad he'd let her in, confided in her, she kissed his chest. "Considering what you just told me about your parents, they're both like you? Or I guess, you're like them? Is this like a family business?"

"Yep, but it didn't start out that way. They wanted me to do anything but this. But life had other plans and I'm not complaining. Though they're more or less retired at this point, at least as far as taking on actual contracts goes."

"So...how did *they* get into the business?"

"That...is a story for another time. Let's just say at one time they worked for the government. And when they got out, they used their skills to join an established outfit. And I was in the Navy, for the record, as well. That's what they wanted for me, but I was never going to be a lifer. And when everything happened with my sister, I stepped into my job more seamlessly than I think they expected."

Elliana blinked as she digested everything he'd told her. "Are they okay with me knowing what they do?"

"The cat's out of the bag now." He shrugged again, as if it didn't matter, and gave her that charming smile that sent heat waves to her core. And he didn't actually answer her question.

"So are you part of a network or something?"

"That I can't answer. Not really. I mean, we don't work alone."

"Are you worried about going to jail or...worse?"

"I've got plans in place in case things ever go sideways. We all do. And if the worst happened and I was caught, my family or associates would break me out of any facility. Sure, I could worry, but there's no point. I live each day the way I want without worrying about extraneous bullshit, and enjoy the people in my life. I don't want to die with regrets."

"Damn," she murmured, beyond impressed and still so curious.

"What?"

"Nothing, I just really like that sentiment." She didn't want to die with regrets either, which was probably why she was so okay with everything he'd told her. Everything he was. Her world had been made up of shades of gray for a long time. "So you really want me to meet your family?"

"Oh yeah. They're dying to meet you. Especially my mom."

She paused. "That sounds ominous."

"No, she's excited because you used to be an explosives expert—"

"There's no 'used to be.'"

He snickered slightly. "Okay, because you are. She wants to talk to you about your preferred choice of explosives and pick your brain."

The very thought had a laugh bubbling up inside Elliana. These sounded like her kind of people. Then she thought of something else. "Do they know about our, uh, late-night activities? With the drone?"

Laughter racking him now, he wrapped his arms around her, burying his face against her head. "Hell no."

She inhaled his masculine scent, wanted to straddle him, take him inside her again, but there was more she needed to ask. She was just having a hard time remembering exactly what those questions were with her face buried against his chest. God, he smelled good.

"So you gonna tell me about your family?" he murmured before she could think of anything else.

He might as well have tossed ice water in her face with how thoroughly that question slapped her. She eased back from his embrace and mumbled an excuse about using the head as she climbed out of bed.

Once she was in the bathroom, she splashed water on her face, then stepped into the small shower. She didn't want to think about, much less talk about her messed-up family.

He might come from a family of killers, but he spoke about them with love and adoration.

She couldn't do the same for hers.

CHAPTER 9

—My ex wasn't an asshole. He was the whole ass.—

Theo waited in the galley for Elliana to come out, not wanting to crowd her. He hadn't dug too much into her past because he didn't want to violate her privacy—more than he already had.

A part of him thought that ship had sailed when she'd started spying on him, but no. That had been consensual. Once he'd realized she'd been watching him for fun, he'd been the one to take things to the next level. Until her, he hadn't realized he liked to be watched either.

Maybe it was because he spent his life in the shadows, always trying not to be seen. But no, it was because it was Elliana doing the watching. He liked that she saw him, all of him, in more ways than one. He could be his authentic self with her, no hiding the core of him.

And now he'd screwed up and wasn't sure how to fix it. He'd never be bringing up her family again, that was for sure.

He glanced over when he heard movement in the front cabin, and like every time he saw her, it was like a punch to the solar plexus when she stepped out.

Her long blonde hair was damp, pulled back into a braid, and she'd put on one of his T-shirts—and nothing else. She might have panties on, but he was choosing to believe she didn't. He forgot to breathe for a moment as he drank in the sight of her lean bare legs. Now that things had changed between them, he could stare all he wanted, drink his fill.

"Sorry about stalking off before," she murmured, heading for the small coffeepot. "My family is a touchy subject."

He shut his laptop as she approached the table. "It's no problem. And I'll never bring them up again."

"No, I want to tell you about them. It's just painful." She snorted softly. "Obviously, or I wouldn't mind talking about it. I'm going to just tell you all of it at once."

"It's fine, you don't need to." Because he could see the pain in her eyes, see it in every inch of her tense body as she sat across from him. And he never wanted to hurt her or inadvertently be the cause of her pain.

"I want to. I don't know what this thing is between us, but I want you to know this about me." She took a breath and looked down at her coffee. "When I was in high school, I dated this guy, who I'll just call Asshole. And he was perfect, or I thought he was. Captain of the baseball team, the guy every girl and some guys wanted."

Oh, Theo wanted to kill this guy already. Hmm, he could add that to his schedule, no problem.

She groaned slightly as she met his gaze. "It's so embarrassing because this story isn't even original. We stayed together while I was in boot camp right after graduation, he wrote me sweet letters, we talked about our future, the kind of house we wanted to buy, where we'd live once I was out. But I'm sure this won't be a surprise—it turns out he was a cheating loser."

"What's his name?" Theo murmured, proud that he kept his tone steady. Casual, even. As if he wasn't plotting the guy's demise.

Elliana gave him a dry look. "Uh, no way. And I know you can find out once I give you more details, but you're not doing anything to him. Trust me, he made his bed and his life sucks now. Anyway, I came home on leave about a year after I'd been in. Our communication hadn't dwindled. He was constantly telling me how much he loved me and couldn't wait to see me. Then when I was home for Christmas, he confessed that he'd been sleeping with my stepsister. And that she was pregnant." She swallowed hard, looked away again.

Theo wanted to pummel the shit out of this guy for causing Elliana an ounce of pain. Pummel him, let his broken bones heal, then pummel him again. But her stepsister? That was unforgivable. "I'm sorry."

"She was pregnant enough that he could and *should* have ended things months before, and saved me the pain of coming home and finding out. It was so bizarre, like my dad and stepmom expected me to just be happy for them. To accept things and we'd all be one happy family.

"Looking back, it's clear he didn't tell them he'd still been in constant contact with me, but they knew he'd cheated on me. My dad felt bad about it, I could tell, but he just expected me to 'make peace with it' as he put it. My stepmom and I never got along, probably because she never wanted me around and I knew it. I was a reminder of the woman who came before her. Because I'm a replica of her." Elliana rolled her eyes, but then seemed to shake it off.

"Anyway, I didn't even unpack, just left and met up with Weston and Van. Got shitfaced, listened to a lot of breakup music, then realized how much better my life was without him. I wouldn't want to be with a cheater anyway, but I reread over some of the emails he'd sent to see if I was crazy, you know? Like if there'd been signs that he'd been pulling away and I just missed them. Because it takes a lot to be screwing someone's sister while still telling them you love them and want a future with them. That's the kind of awful person I'm glad I didn't hitch myself to."

"So earlier, you said that you didn't suspect your family of hiring someone. Why is that?" Because they seemed truly terrible.

She looked away again, her jaw tightening. "My dad is with the Miami PD—not that his job precludes him from hiring someone, but..." Groaning, she looked back at him, winced slightly. "It's embarrassing and I feel like I should have been harsher, but I ended up paying off my dad's mortgage. He'd paid it off before, but then he'd taken a HELOC out on their home because he loaned money to my stepsister." She snorted in disgust. "Of course she never paid him back. I should have just cut contact altogether, and to an extent, I have. My stepsister, ex and stepmom are blocked everywhere. But he's still my dad and that's the house my mom lived in once upon a time. I paid off the mortgage and told him if he ever leveraged the house again, not to bother coming to me."

"Did your stepsister ever contact you?"

Elliana gave him a dry look. "She came looking for money after that *Forbes* article on me came out, no surprise. I did *not* take the high road and ignore her—I might have told her to suck a bag of dicks."

Theo grinned at the bite to her tone. "Good."

She lifted a shoulder, the corner of her mouth curving up ever so slightly. "My ex actually tried to contact me years before that, to apologize for what he'd done and to tell me how miserable he was. As if he thought I'd feel sorry for him, who knows. I never responded and have no regrets. I don't even know what any of them do now. And I don't care.

"I never blocked my dad, but it's been a year since I've talked to him. After I paid off his loan, we never talked." She shrugged, but he could see the pain in her eyes. "And there's a certain amount of pleasure in living my best life, of them having to see my success splashed across the country. Maybe that makes me petty, but I don't care."

He slid around the booth-style seating and took one of her hands in his. "That's not petty, it makes you human. And blood doesn't always make people family."

"I know," she said without hesitation. "Weston and Van are my family. My brothers."

He nodded as he linked his fingers through hers. "I've got blood family and found family too."

"Are they hitmen as well?" she asked, a real smile gracing her face now.

When she smiled it was like the sun came out for a brief moment and everything around them just stopped. "Some." He paused. "Most. Okay, *all* of them."

Now she let out a startled-sounding laugh. "Okay, then."

"Okay?"

"Yep." She looked around at a ringing sound. "Is that my phone?"

"Oh yeah. I hooked it up to the Wi-Fi on the boat," he said as he went to retrieve it from one of the drawers.

"How'd you know my code?"

"You're not the only one who spied. I saw you put it in at one of the HOA meetings."

She snort-laughed again as he handed her the phone. "Now that I know that's not your real house, it's even weirder that you went to the HOA meeting."

He'd only gone to the boring meeting for her, something she should realize. He didn't say anything, however, as she answered her phone.

"Hey, Van. What's up?"

Theo knew exactly who Van Rivers was. Even if he hadn't checked up on Elliana, the man had been in that article with her.

And he was over-the-top handsome in a way even Theo could see. The guy could be starring in movies if he wanted to. Which was why that annoying jealousy popped up as he watched Elliana's expression soften as she talked to him.

"No, I'm fine. I just went offline for a bit, took a little getaway for myself."

There was a pause as she listened to him.

Rolled her eyes. Then, "Oh my god, Weston needs to mind his own business. Is Rebel there with you guys? No, no! Don't put Weston on." She looked at Theo, rolled her eyes again in exasperation and mouthed *nosy chickens.*

Or he thought that was what she'd said. *Chickens?*

"Ah, I...did go on that date." She shot Theo an inscrutable look. "Yep. Yep." She turned away from him and lowered her voice—as if he couldn't still hear her. "I'm not talking about this right now. I'm fine. Uh, nope. Dude, I'm not going to the Christmas Eve party!"

Theo plucked the phone from Elliana, and he was pretty sure he only managed to do it because he'd surprised her. Her blue eyes were wide as he said, "This is Theo, Elliana's new boyfriend. She'll be at the Christmas Eve party and she's bringing me as a plus-one. Also, she's in danger from an unknown threat in the form of an actual contract on her life, so you and your boy Van need to step it up and tighten security at work."

There was a loooonnnng pause, then Weston said, "Please put Elliana back on the phone."

He handed the phone to her, ignoring her glower as she yanked it from his hand, then made her way down into the bedroom cabin.

Theo took the time to pull his own phone out and saw he'd missed a couple calls from his dad. As he started texting him back—seriously, why the phone call, why not just text?—an alert popped up, making him go still.

He'd set up cameras around his house, facing Elliana's, and two had just triggered, one after the other.

After pulling up a full screen on his laptop instead of trying to watch on his phone, he narrowed his gaze as a man in a generic delivery outfit—that looked just similar enough to a well-known company's—strode up to her front door and knocked while holding a small brown package in one hand.

Then the guy rang her doorbell, tried to peer through her front window even though all the blinds were drawn. His head was angled down low enough that Theo doubted the top of the guy's face was caught on Elliana's own front door camera. He'd have to ask her to pull those up once she came back up.

After about thirty seconds, the guy walked away still holding the package, then he did a quick walk along the perimeter of her house on the side that faced Theo's place. He was looking for a way to break in, Theo was certain of it. But he ended up leaving after only a couple minutes, his strides casual as he made his way to the sidewalk then disappeared from sight.

"Is that my house?" Elliana moved in behind him before she slid into the booth next to him.

"Yeah, I've got cameras facing it. This is not a delivery guy." Theo turned the laptop slightly so she could see better.

"I get my stuff delivered to the office anyway. Or my P.O. box," she murmured as she pulled up the app for her security cameras on her phone. "Only got half his face on-screen."

"Download it and send it to me," he said. The angle from her camera was a lot better.

"I don't have your number."

"Yeah you do, I programmed it into your phone."

She snorted as she scrolled down to the T's. "No you didn't."

"It's under 'Best Lover of All Time.'"

She blinked at him, then looked back down at her phone and he could see the way she was fighting a smile. "You've got issues," she muttered, but she smiled and that was all that mattered.

He also noticed that she didn't change the title as she sent him the image in addition to a couple more.

"I'm sending his photo out now to some contacts, going to let them run his face and see what comes up. Until then, there's nothing else to do." Because Theo needed to know who the hitter was before deciding on the next step. And he was more than happy to keep Elliana right where he wanted—safe with him, where no one else knew her location.

"Well, we *could* head back. But first, we're talking about what just happened. You can't just grab my phone like that and take over."

"It didn't seem like you were going to tell them you were in danger."

Her gaze narrowed slightly. "You didn't even give me a chance."

"*Were* you going to tell either of them?"

She gritted her teeth. "It's beside the point."

"Nope. Your safety isn't up for debate." Theo figured that she should know that about him up front; he would always make her safety his number one priority. Clearly—he had cameras pointed at her house and he'd kidnapped her to keep her safe.

"You're just..." She rambled out some nonsensical words, then took a deep breath. "I've literally never wanted to simultaneously punch and kiss someone at the same time."

"I vote for the latter." *Yes, please.*

She let out one of those laughs that made everything in the world right. Then she looked back at the cameras. "Can't believe you've been watching my house."

"No one's going to hurt you." They'd have to go through him first. And luckily, he was hard to kill.

"It's hard to stay mad at you when you're all protective." There was a slight grumble to her words.

"Then don't be mad. Just get naked and let me make you come again."

Her eyes widened in surprise, but then narrowed slightly. "Is sex all you ever think about?"

"When it comes to you, yes." He wasn't sure if he should have been so honest, but he never wanted to lie to her. And when her eyes went molten, he knew that, yep, honesty was definitely the best policy.

"You make me crazy," she murmured. "Just completely out of control."

"We definitely have that in common." He shoved his laptop out of the way, thoughts of the contract and everything pushed to the side as his need for her rose up again. Not that it had actually left to begin with.

She slid out of the booth, pulled his T-shirt over her head, and he'd been right—no panties. In the light of day he saw her clearly, all of her, and knew that this was the woman he was destined to be with.

And he'd never believed in destiny or that shit until her.

Elliana Reed, with a smile like sunshine, a bit of hidden violence inside her, and a capacity for giving that stunned him. She was his future.

He slid out and stood in front of her, hit again by how much smaller she seemed next to him because her presence was like the goddamn sun.

It took him a moment to find his voice as he stared down at the woman who'd gotten under his skin without even trying. "You're mine," he rasped out.

"Yeah?" There was a challenge in her tone as she reached out, not taking her gaze off his, and shoved his pants down with force.

He kept his gaze pinned to hers as he nodded, kicked his pants away. "Yep." He wondered if she understood what he meant, but as she leaned into him, slid her arms around his waist, he forgot to breathe as her breasts pressed against his chest.

A primitive instinct to bind her to him riding him hard, he slid his hand to cup the back of her head and crushed his mouth to hers. The hunger he had for her was like nothing he'd ever expected, an obsession he didn't want to quench.

Instead he leaned into his feelings, especially after she'd trusted him with the truth of her pain. From the moment she'd started watching him, she'd shown him the truth of who she was.

As she teased her tongue against his, he lifted her up, wrapping his hands around the backs of her thighs as he set her on the nearby countertop. He loved the way she spread her legs for him so eagerly, the way she dug her heels into his ass as he pulled her closer.

"I can't get enough of you," he rasped out as he nipped her bottom lip.

She said something, but he couldn't make out the words over the roar of blood in his ears as the need to bring her pleasure overtook him. He was hard between his legs, his erection an insistent reminder of what he wanted.

But she was going to come first, he thought as he teased a finger along her slick folds. "You're already so wet."

"Why do you think I walked out here with just a shirt on?" she panted, sliding her hands down to his ass, clutching tight.

The sound she made as she ran her hands over his back, as if she was memorizing every inch of him, was everything.

"I want more than your fingers now," she whispered, her voice an unsteady rasp.

He stilled for a moment, then pushed another finger inside her, savoring how tight she was. "What is it you want?"

Instead of responding, she reached between their bodies and grasped his erection, stroked him with the kind of pressure he needed. His balls pulled up tight as he pushed into her touch.

"Say the words. Spell it out for me."

A wicked grin spread across her face. "Are you into dirty talk?"

"Apparently," he managed to get out as he began slowly teasing her clit.

She sucked in a breath, her eyes going heavy-lidded for a moment.

"And into voyeurism," he added.

"Technically I'm the one into that," she moaned out as he slid his fingers inside her again. She was so damn slick and it was all for him. "But only for you."

"That's right, you'll only ever watch me," he growled out as possessiveness swept through him, consumed him.

She spread her legs wider as he guided himself to her entrance. Not that he even needed the help of his hand, his cock knew exactly where it wanted to go.

"Theo," she practically shouted in surprise as he thrust all the way inside her. Then she wrapped her legs around his waist, held tight, held him in place as she lifted her face to his again.

He cupped one of her breasts, began slowly teasing its hardened bud as he claimed her mouth. As he teased her sensitive nipple, he stayed buried inside her, his cock pulsing with need, just the sensation of being enveloped by her tight body making all his muscles pull taut.

She nipped his bottom lip as she ground out, "Move!"

He smiled against her mouth, loving her impatience. Instead of moving, he reached between their bodies with his free hand and rubbed her clit again in tight little circles.

She rolled her hips against him, trying to force him to move, but in this position he was the one in control. Though who was he kidding—she was always in control where he was concerned.

And each time she tried to force him to move, he felt her inner walls tighten even harder around him. He was going to push her right to the edge, then when she started coming, he'd start moving.

She dug her fingers into his ass with impatience. "Theo, move, please." The words came out like a plea.

Oh, and he liked the sound of her begging, the sound of her desperate for him. He moved ever so slightly, barely pulling back before he thrust again.

She bit his bottom lip, dug her fingernails into him now. "You're a monster."

He laughed against her mouth even as he began teasing her clit harder, in the little pattern she'd seemed to love last night. Or this morning. He barely knew what day it was. "You love it."

She simply moaned in response, her inner walls clenching faster now. And he knew she was close.

The moment her orgasm started to build, when those little ripples around his cock turned to milking him, he pulled back and began thrusting inside her, prolonging her climax with each pump. With each deep thrust.

"Theo!" The way she called out his name was pure music, wrapping around him, imprinting on him.

And as her orgasm started to ebb, as her lean body began to grow lax, he finally let go of his own control. He'd barely been hanging on anyway.

He continued pumping, harder now, completely losing himself inside her as he marked her, claimed her.

Elliana was the woman he'd never realized he needed in his life. And he wasn't letting her go.

Chapter 10

—I found my North Star.—

Hours later, Elliana looked at the short list of people she'd come up with who might hate her enough to want her dead, but everyone on the list was a stretch, all competitors. And so far it didn't seem as if Van or Weston or anyone else at work had been targeted. Nothing that she or Theo could find.

"This list is crap," she muttered, but took the glass of water Theo handed her as he slid onto the seat next to her.

They were on the back deck now, the sun bright in the sky, but there was enough cloud cover that it wasn't blinding. And the water itself was a gorgeous dark blue that stretched all around them, the small waves like glittering jewels. Because of the size of the boat, it seemed to temper most of the waves because she barely felt the subtle shifting.

"I agree, because I've already looked into all of them." He frowned at her screen. "What about anyone you've fired recently? An assistant, or someone who didn't like working for a female boss."

His words gave her pause, but then she shook them off. "My assistant is a woman and she's amazing, so she's out."

Theo's gaze narrowed slightly. "You paused though. I already looked into your personal assistant and I agree that she seems solid. But I saw the pause."

"Oh, not because of her. It's so stupid I don't even want to bring it up."

But Theo watched her with those tiger eyes, his muscular arm stretched out across the back of the cream-colored cushion on the bench seating as he watched her. Waited.

"Fine. A couple months ago, we—meaning, me, Van *and* Weston—interviewed someone for one of our executive positions. The man came highly recommended and has a lot of pertinent experience. On paper he seemed perfect. But once we got to the interview part, he only looked at Van and Weston when answering. I won't get into the whole thing, but he acted like I was window dressing." She lifted a shoulder because she'd dealt with subtle and not-so-subtle sexism her entire life. Hell, she'd been the only woman in her unit when she'd been in the Marines.

"You obviously didn't hire him." Theo's eyes had gone flinty now, the predator come out to play.

She snorted softly. "Um, no. And he was *so* sure he was getting that job, acting as if it was a formality to be interviewed. Don't get me wrong, the guy really is talented, but he was the wrong fit for our culture. Van wanted me to be the one to send him the rejection, because he's got a little bit of petty in him too." Elliana grinned now. "I sent out a professional, polite rejection email letting him know we were going in another direction, but we enjoyed speaking with him, blah, blah, blah, and he did not handle it well."

"How so?"

"He responded with a snarky reply that actually surprised me. At first I thought he just reacted poorly and made a stupid decision to respond to a rejection. Not the best, but he's human so I let it go and put it out of my mind. But he messaged me again a few weeks later because he thought I got him blacklisted or something from the industry, when he wasn't hired for another job with a similar company. I had no clue what he was talking about and made it clear that he shouldn't contact me again. After that, a few Glassdoor reviews popped up targeting me specifically. Clearly fake, but I let it go. Though the three of us did put him on an internal 'never interview or hire list' for the future. But that's it."

"Some men have fragile egos."

"Enough to hire a hitman though? That's just *so* extreme." She shook her head, even as she remembered how annoyed she'd been during that interview. The man had looked right through her when he'd answered questions. The couple of times he'd looked at her at all. "And he comes from money so it's not like he's struggling. The guy is loaded."

"What's his name?"

After she told him, she pulled up James Gillen online and started looking into his financials using less-than-official means. AKA she put her hacking skills to good use. Because screw this guy. She might have put him out of her mind, but he'd been truly awful, so maybe...just maybe he was behind this.

Theo was at his own computer, his fingers flying across the keyboard as he worked.

"I'm digging into his financials. What are you doing?" she murmured as she found what looked like normal bank accounts, retirement accounts, a vacation house listed in the man's name. He came from serious generational wealth, had gone to all Ivy League schools, and had recently moved from the West Coast to the East Coast.

"Now that I have a name, I'm tossing it out to a few of my associates to see if it's familiar. I actually do recognize his name from a couple business journal articles, but I don't know anything about him other than he used to live in California."

"I'm sending the info to Van and Weston, just so they know who we're looking into—since you narced me out to them."

Theo's expression was purely unapologetic. "I'll never apologize for letting your family know you're in danger."

She grumbled to herself, then turned back to what was actually important. "So far Gillen's financials look normal enough." Though she was pretty sure he was hiding some money in the Caymans. But the deeper she dug, the more she realized this guy had secret accounts.

"He cheated on his first wife," Theo said into the calm of the two of them working.

She liked being with him like this, even with the weird circumstances. Liked how relaxed he was and didn't need to fill the silence. Because it was a comfortable silence as they both worked. "Shocker," she muttered. "And he's definitely hiding money from his ex-wife. So I'm going to anonymously send her some information," she said, still working away.

"She's got a similar look as you. Tall, blonde," he added. "Could be what triggered him to act like a fool in the interview with you."

She shrugged, not really caring about the why of it. The entitled didn't normally need a reason. As she looked at her screen, scanning some recent withdrawals, she paused. They were all made around the same time, but from different accounts. "How much was the contract on me again? Not the bitcoin, but the cash." She remembered, but she wanted to confirm the number, to make sure what she was seeing was correct.

After Theo told her, she turned her screen around to show him, her eyes wide with shock. The amount withdrawn from the multiple accounts all added up to the final payment on the contract. "I...I think he might be the guy."

Chapter 11

—If you're lucky enough to find your weirdo, don't let them go.—

Theo wasn't sure how to handle Elliana's quiet as he guided them back to the marina. As a rule, he didn't mind quiet. If anything, he relished it as a part of his profession. But she hadn't been talking much since he'd pulled up the anchor and they'd started the ride back. She'd worked on her computer for a while, but had finally put it away and was now sitting next to him as they cut across the Atlantic, only twenty minutes out from docking.

"I think I'm going to bake some bread, or maybe a lemon loaf for the Christmas Eve party," he said, cutting into the quiet. Because he desperately wanted to hear her voice. At this point he was addicted to it—he was addicted to all of her.

She glanced at him, surprise clear on her face. "You bake bread?"

"Yeah, why?"

"You're a hitman," she sputtered. "You can't bake bread."

He laughed at her words. "I'm pretty sure it's not in our employee handbook but I'll double check to make sure I can."

She paused, blinked once... "Is there really a handbook?"

Shaking his head, he barked out a laugh and turned back to driving, watching the wide video screen as he approached the marina. This thing was top-of-the-line and he could see exactly where he was going from the interior cabin's steering. "Not that I know of, but I'll check. Oh, I'll bring a nice bottle of wine to complement the bread."

Maybe he shouldn't push about the party, but it seemed clear that the reason she hated Christmas was her ex. Or at least part of the reason. The asshole had revealed his cheating on her Christmas break one year. Wasn't hard to put it together.

"I don't even know if we'll be able to go," she murmured. "Not with so much in the air." She stood up then and moved through the cabin toward the back of the boat. "And Van and Weston are still blowing up my phone, thanks to you."

Yep, still not apologizing for that. And he didn't like her pulling away from him, didn't like her physically away from him either. He wanted to handcuff her to him all the time. Which wasn't possible. Right?

He shook his head as the radio sounded, and responded to the dockmaster at the dock as he slowed his entrance. "There's a ball cap hanging in the main cabin. Will you wear it when we disembark?"

"Uh, sure." She headed past him, her clothes casual, the oversized sweater she was wearing a simple blue and white over her dark jeans. He'd asked his friend who'd stocked the boat to pack some things and, as usual, the man had come through.

She came back up and had her long blonde hair tucked under the cap and a pair of dark Gucci sunglasses on as well. He wasn't sure whose they were, as his entire family used this yacht from time to time. For work and play. But usually work, as it was an easy way to travel undetected.

"For any CCTV cameras, right?" she asked as she settled next to him again.

“Yep. We’re going to stop this guy,” he added as he reached out, squeezed her hand.

“I know. I...it’s just a lot to process. It’s so random and psychotic. Weston and Van are on the same page, by the way. Even without the bank account stuff, they think Gillen is a bad apple.”

In his experience, the world was full of psychos, and people died from random shit every day. So this wasn’t as shocking to him as it was to her. But he kept that to himself—and he was glad her two partners, who were more brothers than anything, agreed. “We’ll head back to my real home. Is there anything specific you need from your house?”

“Ah, that bag of stuff down there is fine but yeah, later I’d like to grab some stuff. Namely my shampoo and conditioner. And my hair dryer,” she tacked on.

“Oh, I have a hair dryer, I think.” Or he was pretty sure he did.

She snort-laughed, the sound adorable. “Trust me, yours isn’t like mine. You probably have one of those drugstore kinds.” And the way she said that was as if it was a sin.

Now he was curious about her damn hair dryer. “What’s special about yours?”

She shrugged, but all she said was, “It’s magic.”

“You and my sister are going to get along great,” he murmured as he finally steered to a stop. Because she was obsessive over her hair dryer and diffuser too. Wouldn’t go on vacation without them.

He talked into the radio as he grabbed both their bags from below, then stepped out on the back deck first, looking around for any potential threat.

“Mr. Johnson, good to see you again.” Ramon, the dockmaster, greeted him by his pseudonym as the team on the dock started tying off the beast of a boat. They’d wash it as well, and there was a cleaning crew that would come in tomorrow or the day after to straighten up things.

"Likewise." He made small talk as he and Elliana disembarked. She remained quiet as she texted, but once they were in his waiting SUV she set her phone down and let out a sigh of relief.

"I didn't really feel the waves, but my legs feel a little wobbly now that we're back on dry land."

His legs were a lot wobbly, but that was metaphorically, because of her. She'd turned his life upside down and he didn't want his previous one back. He only wanted a future with her. "I've been thinking about how we bring Gillen down."

She paused. "You mean...kill him?"

"It's the best option." Because the man wouldn't be going to jail. The bastard would still have access to the outside world, could try to hurt Elliana again. And there was no world in which Theo allowed a present danger against Elliana to exist.

"There's got to be a better way. Jail would be worse for someone like him," she muttered. "He's had everything handed to him, and even with all that, his ego is so fragile he can't take a professional rejection. It's pathetic. Rich prick."

And once again it amused him how she didn't think of herself as wealthy. From his research, her day-to-day spending habits had barely changed. The only difference was that she seemed to be giving away huge chunks of her money. When he'd started looking into her, he'd found that she'd given an entire senior class scholarships for college. No stipulations about grades, nothing. Just paid for their first year. And there hadn't been any press about it, which told him that she needed a better PR person. Not that he thought she was doing it for glory or whatever, but still. The world should know how amazing she was.

When Theo's phone buzzed, he glanced at it briefly but didn't pull up the whole message even though he was at a stoplight. Because it was from his father, and he could see part of the message—giving the current location of James Gillen, the man who wanted his Elliana dead.

The bastard who was going to die.

"I like this part of Miami." Elliana's voice was soft as she looked out the window, the sun fading in the sky already.

"Me too. I grew up here, by the way."

She looked over in surprise. "Really?"

"Yep."

"Huh, so we're both Miami natives." She gave him another one of those heart-stopping smiles before she looked back out the window. "Even though I totally hate Christmas, I love the way the city is all lit up and so...soft-looking, I guess. Maybe that's the wrong word, but everything has a sort of glow right now."

She wasn't wrong. There were lights everywhere they drove, on practically every place of business, and now as they went deeper into an established neighborhood with huge yards and space between houses, the majority of homes had Christmas decorations, with a handful of Hanukkah ones. As a whole, their neighborhood loved a good party. And almost everyone on his particular street was a hitman. Something he probably should have told Elliana.

"Oh my god," she breathed out as they reached the end of the cul-de-sac. "Is yours the one with the giant Grinch on the roof?"

He simply grinned at the two-story brick home he'd owned the last four years. "Yep."

She muttered something to herself he didn't quite make out as he pulled into his garage, shutting it behind them. "So when are we going after him? What's the plan?" she finally demanded as she blurted the questions. "I need more information because it's driving me crazy thinking of someone out there gunning for me. For no reason, I might add."

"I have a couple ideas but I wanted to go over everything with you first." But at the end of the day, Gillen was going to die. He just wasn't certain she'd be okay with that outcome.

"Okay, I'm ready to get this done. I want my life back."

He just hoped that life included him. "Come on, let's get inside. You need dinner and wine." Maybe it would make her more amenable to his murder plan.

"Modern but homey," she murmured, looking around his renovated kitchen.

Everything was sleek and shiny, mostly grays and whites, but he liked to cook during his nonwork hours so it was a well-used kitchen. Not to mention his niece Nessa was over a lot and there was evidence of her drawings on his refrigerator, among other things—like one of her handheld gaming systems tossed in the bowl with apples.

"We can order takeout or I could cook. Are you in the mood for Italian? I could whip up some chicken parm." He knew she liked Italian from the food deliveries she'd gotten over the last year.

"Really?" She slid onto one of the stools at the island top.

"Yep. I love to cook. And we can talk about the plan."

"Okay. Do you want help..." Trailing off, she paused at the same time he did at the sound of the doorbell.

He glanced at his phone screen as the incoming alert dinged, then winced as he saw his niece and sister on his doorbell camera. Nessa was sticking her tongue out at it as his sister put her hand on the biometric scanner. "I wasn't planning on this," he hurried out. "But my sister and niece are here." And they always had access. He'd never had a reason to want a heads-up—until now.

"Oh." A hint of panic bled into Elliana's eyes as she glanced around—to escape, maybe?

"Uncle Theo!" a young female voice shouted moments before Nessa raced into the room, her curly red hair flying out behind her. But she froze as she saw Elliana, her green eyes going wide. "Who are you?"

"This is Elliana," Theo said as he moved to stand next to her, wrapping an arm around her shoulders.

Moments later his sister strode in behind her, *her* green eyes widening as well, but she smiled as she greeted Elliana. "Hi, I'm Theo's sister, Aileen."

"It's nice to meet you both." Elliana was a little stiff, but she was smiling between the two of them.

"Are you my uncle's girlfriend? You're super pretty!" Nessa blurted.

Elliana's eyes widened. "Ah..."

"Yes," Theo answered quickly. "She's my girlfriend. And what's that you've got there?" He motioned to the big box she was carrying.

Attention on Elliana gone, Nessa looked down at the brown box and held it up. "Grandpa got me a new drone, but it's too hard to figure out. I saw you drive up and I need your help. Pleeeasssseee!"

"I've got to start dinner but Elliana is a pro with drones." That being an understatement. "I bet she'll help you if you ask nicely."

Green gaze once again riveted on Elliana, she said. "You'll help?"

"Ah, sure." Looking only a little lost, she glanced at Theo. "Your backyard is...good?"

Meaning safe. "Yep. I've got cameras and alerts back there." Not that anyone could know where Elliana was.

"Okay, then. Let's goooo." Nessa, who'd never met a stranger, grabbed Elliana's hand and dragged her out of the kitchen, already talking about how cool her new present was.

"A drone?" he murmured once he heard the back door shut. Then he turned his tablet on so he had a clear view of the backyard cameras.

"They're giving her a present a night up until Christmas." Aileen's voice was dry as she sat at the countertop next to where Elliana had been sitting.

"Looks like they gave you one too. Nice earrings." He let out a low whistle, because damn. Those were definitely expensive.

"These aren't from you?" She touched the huge emeralds in her ears.

"Uh, *no*. Not that I don't love you but it'd be weird if I got you jewelry." Especially something clearly at least ten grand. That was like a husband-level gift. And at that thought, Theo had an idea of who might have given them to her but kept it to himself. Because his sister was blind where a certain someone was concerned.

"Oh…" She touched her ears absently again, then shook her head. "So, Elliana huh? She's now your girlfriend?"

He shrugged as he started pulling out all the ingredients, glad he'd thawed out chicken before he'd kidnapped his now girlfriend, soon to be more. Maybe they could just skip the whole fiancée thing and jump right to wife.

Wife. Yep, he liked the sound of that.

"So what does she think you actually do for a living?" his sister asked, cutting into his train of thought.

"She knows the truth."

"Ooooh. Wow." Aileen blinked once. Twice. Then she went to his pantry and pulled out a bottle of red. "Okay, so holy shit, Theo. Dad said something about it but he was kind of vague. And honestly, I thought he was full of it. Oh my god!" she exclaimed as she pulled the cork out.

"What?"

"This is huge and you're so calm about it! You have a girlfriend who's totally gorgeous and knows what you do! And is clearly okay with it. Isn't she like your dream woman? How are you not freaking out?"

He shrugged again as he started pounding the chicken breasts. "I've got more important things to worry about. Like someone wanting my woman dead." He briefly told his sister what was going on, right down to who they suspected had put out the hit.

Aileen took a big sip of her wine as he finished. "That's a lot. I bet this is so hard on her," she added, glancing at the tablet and smiling as Nessa squealed at something Elliana did. "Nessa sure likes her, which is a plus."

"Of course she does. Elliana's perfect."

His sister snort-laughed as she set her glass down. “Oh, you’ve got it so bad.”

Yep, and he didn’t care.

***

“Oh. My. God.” Nessa stomped back into the kitchen holding the remote control and small drone in both hands. “Mom! You’ll never believe what we saw on the drone. Mr. Richards was kissing *Mrs.* Baker in between their houses. And not like a peck on the cheek! There was tongue involved.” She made a barfing sound, very much grossed out by the thought of that.

Elliana hadn’t been sure who they were, but Nessa had informed her of everyone’s identity in a five-block radius as she spied on her neighbors. Apparently Mr. Richards owned a couple ice cream shops and Mrs. Baker was a vice principal at a local high school. And she was married to “Mean Mr. Baker.” So Nessa didn’t seem to particularly care that she was kissing someone else.

Aileen’s eyes went wide as she plucked up the drone from her daughter. “We’re going to have to talk about rules and boundaries when using this thing.”

Nessa shrugged, then gave Elliana a surprise hug. “Thanks for showing me so much. I hope I get to see you again soon.”

“I hope I do too.” She found herself smiling down at the talkative ten-year-old. The redhead had been nonstop since they’d stepped outside, telling her about her classmates, her grandparents, her uncle Theo, and a bunch of other stuff Elliana had only half heard.

“And thank you for the advice about what to do at school.”

Elliana nodded again, smiling as Theo placed a glass of wine in her hand.

"What advice?" Theo asked.

"Oh, just soccer stuff. I've got my painting class, Mom! And I don't want to be late. Especially since we were late last week."

Elliana lifted her glass of wine to cover her smile at the gimlet eye Nessa gave her mom.

"Heaven forbid we're ever a few minutes late." Aileen shook her head slightly.

"If you're not early, you're late!" both Nessa and Theo said in unison.

Aileen gave Elliana a dry look. "You see what I have to live with?"

Elliana just snickered as the two of them headed out, Nessa talking away about what she was going to paint this week.

"You played soccer?" Theo asked.

"In high school." Elliana grinned as she added, "And in Afghanistan. Van and Weston always wanted me on their team."

"So what advice did you give Nessa?"

To his surprise, Elliana's cheeks tinged a faint shade of pink. "Some girl's been messing with her, so I mentioned that if she kicks her right here in the shin," she said, pointing, "during soccer, it'll get her off her back. She can play it off like it was just a soccer thing and avoid getting in trouble. But in hindsight, maybe that's not the best advice."

Oh, she was going to get along just fine with his family. "Sounds good to me. But definitely don't tell my sister."

"So...the plan?" Elliana asked.

"My dad has a location on Gillen. Which helps us. He's in Orlando for the next few days, likely giving himself an alibi. Has been posting pictures of himself all over social media at different functions."

"What about the guy who picked up the contract?"

"We've got his name now too."

"Is he a pro?"

"Yeah. Professional, always finishes the job." Which was just a giant pain in the ass. It would have made things a lot easier if the guy had hired an amateur. But Gillen had changed the parameters of the contract, something Theo didn't want to think about, much less tell Elliana. It was important, however, and he had to tell her because it shifted his original plan. "But things have changed. Gillen doesn't want you killed. He wants you brought to him, alive."

"What? Why..." She trailed off for a moment. "Wait, to kill me *himself?*"

"And likely worse. There's no way he wants you just to kill you." Theo's hands automatically balled into fists, but he took a steadying breath. A man like Gillen was weak, pathetic. He'd want to hurt her, torture her.

Instead of fear, rage rolled off Elliana then. "Oh, we're taking this guy down. I know you want to kill him, but I'm telling you jail will be a hell of a lot worse. We can bring him down, I know it!"

"Before we can take down Gillen, we've got to eliminate the hitter first. Then I'll pose as him and 'deliver' you to Gillen." That was when Theo would blow his brains out. He wouldn't torture him, even though the bastard deserved it. But Gillen wasn't walking away.

"Okay, that's a good idea...but how do we bring down the hitter? Or find him or whatever?"

Theo scrubbed a hand over his face as he ran through scenarios. "This particular hitter is known for two things—car bombs or making someone's death look like a suicide. Since we know he now wants to bring you in alive, he'll be careful, will try to take you while you're alone. I think the best plan will be for you to return to your house, as if you're coming back from a short getaway, then head to the office before he can break into your place. He'll follow you and either try to take you on the road or at the office."

"The office is a ghost town right now. No one's working on-site until the new year. I'll have to tell Van and Weston though..." She trailed off, frowning.

"Is that a bad thing? They both love you and they're trained."

"No, it's not bad, exactly. I just... I don't want to bring them into this. It feels like too many people will be involved, and Weston has Rebel now. I just... Can I think on this?"

"Of course. But you know we'll have to bring my family into this. Because I'm not letting you out of my sight. And I'm not letting this asshole take you because we weren't prepared properly. So we won't do it tonight. I want to start fresh, tomorrow morning."

"Okay."

"Okay?"

"Well, yeah. They're clearly trained. And so am I, for the record. So don't think you'll be, like...handcuffing me again for my own good or anything."

Grinning, he rounded the island countertop. "Handcuffing you doesn't seem all bad."

Laughing lightly, she grabbed his T-shirt and tugged him down to her. "Maybe I'll handcuff you to my bed next time," she murmured before he crushed his mouth to hers.

Heat and hunger surged through him as he tasted the woman he'd fallen for. Because this had changed from obsession into something more solid. Something that felt a lot like forever.

Chapter 12

—He's the plot twist I didn't see coming.—

"I don't want to get up," Elliana grumbled, turning her face into Theo's bare chest.

At this point everything was bare between them. In more ways than one, and she was terrified to accept that they might have a future. She'd been closed off for so long, to the possibility of letting anyone in romantically, that it was comfortable to keep those walls around her. And considering someone wanted her dead right now, she figured it was fine to worry about only that and figure out the relationship stuff later.

"Five more minutes, then we've got to get moving." He kissed the top of her head as he pulled the covers up higher over them.

His room was fairly "guy basic," as she thought of it. There was a huge bed, a giant television on the wall, and dark furniture. There were a few pieces of art on the walls but they were sort of generic, as if he hadn't put much thought into them. Or maybe they'd come with the house? At least he had a big stack of books on his nightstand.

Inhaling his dark scent, she snuggled up against him. The man was like a furnace and she could go right back to sleep if he'd just let her.

"What do you want for Christmas?" he murmured into the comfortable quiet of the darkened room.

She jolted slightly at the question, surprised he was thinking about anything but the asshole who wanted her dead. "I don't want a Christmas present. I don't really do them."

"Hmm, well I do. So I'll just have to guess, then."

She gently pinched him in the side. "Why are you being so pushy about this dumb holiday when we've got important things to worry about?" Like baiting a hitman into coming after her.

"Because I don't think it actually is dumb to you. I think you got hurt around Christmas and now you pretend to hate it. And because I'm a bulldozer sometimes, according to my sister."

"Bulldozer is a perfect description," she agreed. "Fine, what do *you* want for Christmas then?"

"You."

Laughing, she looked up at him. "That's not a real answer."

"It's the only one you're getting. Well, and I want Gillen dead. So that's two presents. But you're all I need."

"You can't give me a dead body as a gift." Especially of a guy who belonged in prison, watching the years pass him by, having all his luxuries taken away from him.

He shrugged. "I beg to differ."

After a long pause, she said, "My mom loved Christmas. Like, really loved it. She used to call me her Christmas Sunshine. And apparently she'd wanted to actually name me something Christmas themed—maybe even Christmas—but my dad convinced her not to."

He wrapped his arms tighter around her, kissed the top of her head. "She sounds amazing."

"She was. And when she died, everything changed." Even her dad had changed, had morphed into someone she didn't like much as he twisted himself into something different for his new wife. Elliana didn't even think of her as her stepmom anymore. She was just someone Elliana didn't like and never wanted in her life.

It felt strange to open up to Theo because, well, it *didn't* feel so strange. It almost felt natural, and that knowledge shifted everything inside her. He was just supposed to be this hot neighbor she appreciated from afar. But now everything was so different than she ever could have imagined. This thing between her and Theo was very real.

"I'm going to take a shower. Want to join me?" he murmured, his tone low and inviting.

And warmth spread through her immediately. She looked up at him and dropped a kiss on his mouth before she slid out of bed. The sex between them was good. Better than good—it was incredible with him. And it gave her something to think about other than the guy who wanted her dead and the future with Theo she was terrified to think about too hard.

"I'm going to make some coffee but I'll join you in a couple minutes. So don't start anything without me." Grabbing his discarded T-shirt from the floor, she tugged it over her head and made her way to the kitchen.

But when she got there, she realized they weren't alone in the house.

CHAPTER 13

—Order doesn't equal justice.—

"I'm sorry, but C-4 is the superior choice." Elliana's voice rang out from his kitchen as Theo approached on silent feet. She'd never joined him in the shower and now he was beyond cranky.

He wasn't certain who she was talking to but he had a good idea. His mother had figured out a way to sneak into his house—"to teach you how to implement better security protocols"—and he still hadn't figured out how she was doing it.

"Semtex has far more raw power." Yep, that was his mother, in her all-knowing tone.

"Well sure, but C-4 is a lot more stable and that's incredibly important when transporting. And for accuracy. We can just agree to disagree because C-4 will always be my first choice."

"Fine, we'll just disagree, then. But clearly you have good taste in men because you're at my son's house. So, what is going on between you two? Because Nessa said you're his girlfriend."

There was a looong pause, during which Theo was really curious what Elliana's answer would be.

But when she cleared her throat, fake coughed, then said, “Um...” he stepped inside.

“Mom, how nice of you to drop by *uninvited*.” He grinned as he approached the petite redhead who’d taught him to make his first explosive on his ninth birthday. (His mother might deny that she’d wanted him to follow in her footsteps, but stuff like that made him wonder.)

His mother grinned as she turned to face him.

Elliana smiled as well, and she actually looked relaxed, which surprised him. Their discussion had sounded good-natured but he’d never brought a woman home before. And he’d never introduced anyone to his parents. Ever.

And he knew his parents could be a lot. Hell, *he* was a lot.

“My sweet boy,” she said with a smile. “Tell me, which do you prefer, C-4 or Semtex?”

“I prefer to never answer that question.” He kissed his mom’s cheek before he moved in next to Elliana, wrapping a protective arm around her shoulders as he looked down at what the two women had been poring over. “So...what the hell is this?” He motioned to the mini blueprints on the countertop. “You robbing a bank now?”

His mother shook her head, her red curls bouncing slightly. “Please, that’s child’s play. These are the blueprints to the house Gillen is staying at. One of his family’s homes.”

“Your mom thinks we should blow his house up, drive him out, scare him. While I’m a little hesitant, I like the idea of him being terrified for his life.” That fire was in Elliana’s gaze as she looked up at him. “And I do enjoy blowing things up.”

“That’s one idea.” He kissed the top of her head, because he needed to be touching her constantly. “But this isn’t what Dad and I discussed.” This had chaos written all over it. Right now, that was the last thing they wanted. “And it’s going to bring a lot of attention. Which means an investigation,” he added, looking pointedly at his mom. They didn’t go around blowing shit up on a regular basis so he wasn't sure what was going on with her. Unless she maybe just wanted to bond with Elliana? "We're sticking to the plan."

His mom sniffed in annoyance before she slid off her stool. "Fine. We're ready to go. Just let me know when you are." Her expression softened when she looked at Elliana. "In case my son hasn't invited you over yet, I hope we'll see you for Christmas dinner. And Boxing Day, of course."

"Ah...okay, thank you. I'll be there. Did you want me to bring anything?"

"Just your lovely self." She clasped Elliana's hands in hers once before shooting Theo a look he couldn't even begin to decipher, then strode out the front door, setting off the alarm as she went.

"Hold on," he muttered as he went to disarm it. "Did you see her get in? I still can't figure out how she's bypassing the system."

She snorted softly. "Uh, no. She was waiting in the kitchen. And for the record, I like her, but she's also terrifying. She told me this story about her and your dad when they pulled a job in Beirut and how they ended up killing someone who betrayed them. It was shockingly detailed. I can't be sure, but I'm pretty sure she was threatening me." Elliana was looking at him for confirmation, her blue eyes searching his.

Theo shook his head as he pulled her into his arms, claiming her mouth in a long, lingering kiss because very soon they needed to leave to lure the hitter out of hiding so they could take the bastard down.

And move to the next stage. Which was where things got tricky. Because Elliana didn't want him killing Gillen. And Gillen needed to die. It was a puzzle he was still trying to figure out.

"She wasn't threatening you," he said as he pulled away. "She liked you, trust me." His mom wouldn't have bothered to stick around and discuss explosives if she hadn't liked Elliana. And she definitely wouldn't have invited her to Christmas dinner. That was for family only. "But we're going to forget everything about blowing up Gillen's place."

Elliana grumbled slightly. "I'll put a pin in it, but I'm not forgetting it. The more I think about all this, the angrier I get. Everything I've found on this guy points to him being a horrible human. Something we didn't find in our background check before we interviewed him. The dig we did was deep but it was a professional one, not a personal one. And this guy has a reputation for cheating on all the women he's been with, for getting good employees fired from various establishments. He even fired the woman who'd been cleaning his house for decades with no warning, cutting off her health insurance right when she'd been primed to retire. He's just a big pile of garbage."

"Hold on to that anger and use it. Can you be ready in an hour?"

She nodded, slid off the stool. "I can be ready sooner. So, I'm driving to my place, grabbing some stuff inside and then driving to the office?"

"Yep. My father is already at my house—my temporary one next to yours—keeping an eye on your place. Someone is definitely watching your house, even if we can't see them. So they'll know when you're home. I need you to leave almost immediately so there's no chance of him trying to take you at your house."

"Why don't we want to do this at my house? Why go to my office?"

"Because it's bigger and quieter." And if he was being totally honest, he didn't want to kill someone where she felt safe. Didn't want to contaminate her domain. "And I'll be able to get into place and wait. Not to mention we'll be able to basically lead him exactly where we want him to go, control everything."

She nodded slowly and bit her bottom lip in the most adorable way. "Okay. I just worry he'll get suspicious when there's no physical security at the office."

"It's a risk we'll have to take." It was the weakest part of the plan, having her send the security people home.

“No.” Elliana shook her head. “It’s too risky, Theo. Way too suspicious. We should do this at my place, let him confront me there. It allows for less margin of error anyway. I go home and basically wait for him. One stop. And we avoid the risk that he tries to grab me while I’m driving, because you can’t control that. You can get into my house without being seen, right?”

“Yeah,” he grumbled, knowing she was right. Had been thinking the same thing. “There’s a risk that he’ll see me sneaking into your place ahead of you. And...I simply don’t want to do this at your house. It’s where you sleep at night, your domain.”

She strode toward him, still wearing his T-shirt, though it was more like a dress on her. “I appreciate that, but I think this is the best way. You said you have a good...clean-up crew, right?” She seemed to struggle with the words.

But he nodded. “Yeah. Quick and very efficient.” They knew how to clean up blood and forensic evidence so cleanly that even if a forensics team came in, they’d find nothing out of the ordinary.

“Let’s do this, then.” She reached for him as she said the words, wrapped her arms around him tight and buried her face against his chest. “Then we go after Gillen.”

Oh, they’d be going after that bastard all right. Gillen wasn’t going to see this Christmas.

CHAPTER 14

—Actions, meet consequences.—

Elliana hated waiting, but knew the wait was almost over. The roman shades behind her were partially down as she sat at her home desk and did nothing but stare at her blank computer screen and wait for a killer to try to kidnap her.

Because that was how she spent her days off now.

"He's in." The quiet voice of Theo's mother sounded in Elliana's well-hidden earpiece. "Walked up on foot so he must have been staying in a nearby home. He's dressed in a delivery uniform."

Elliana had left her security system off and hoped the guy wouldn't think it was strange. It was the middle of the day and most of her neighbors were home because of the holidays, so who would be expecting a robbery now? Or more specifically, a kidnapping for a deranged client with a stupidly fragile ego?

She heard a ghost of sound as she clicked on her keyboard, keeping up the appearance of doing work. She jolted slightly when a man dressed in a generic delivery uniform with a balaclava over his face stepped inside, weapon out. Even with the warning, it was a shock to see a stranger in her home. Much less a masked one. The mask gave him an extra sense of menace.

Before she could even think about responding to the intrusion, he pointed his weapon at her—but then froze as he eyed the block of C-4 on her desk. His body language was cautious, but his weapon hand never wavered. The C-4 had been her idea. Because otherwise, what was stopping the guy from simply attacking her and restraining her? She'd needed a way to give him pause, so she could talk to him. To try to negotiate. Though Theo thought it was a waste of time, she wanted to at least try.

"Hands where I can see them and get on the ground, then put your hands behind your back." His voice was icy calm, but his eyes flicked to the block of C-4 again.

It was simply an inert block of explosives, couldn't do anything without a detonator. Something he would know. But the sight of it had clearly surprised him, which was entirely the point. She wanted to talk to him before Theo went all hitman on him. Wanted to see if they could defuse this situation and get him to turn on the man who'd hired him.

Elliana stretched back in her chair, crossed her legs as she eyed the man in the balaclava. "Nah, I'm good, but thanks."

The man's entire body language changed at her quick nope. He'd moved into her office like an operator at first, and according to Theo, he was. But she had two things on her side right now. One, she knew that this guy wanted her brought to Gillen alive. And two, Theo was standing behind her door, waiting to take him down.

"Get the fuck up, now," he ordered, taking a step toward her.

She pulled out her own weapon, pointed it at him. "How about no and I have a counteroffer? I pay you double what the bastard who hired you is paying, to walk away. Simple and easy. You take the money and call it a day. Easy work."

He paused and it was clear he was thinking it over, but then he straightened. "I do something like that and I'll get a reputation for not finishing my jobs. That'll hurt my future work so it's not worth the temporary money. Besides," he added, moving a step closer, the look in his eyes darkening, "you're the hottest piece of ass I've seen in a long time. I'm going to enjoy you before I turn you over. Because he was very clear that I could damage the merchandise as long as I don't kill you."

Oh, that was the *wrong* thing to say. Theo moved quicker than she could have imagined, stepping out from behind the door like a wraith. Then the *puff puff* of his silencer as he shot the guy in the head twice.

He shot again as he approached on silent feet, clearly not done as he emptied his pistol into the guy's back.

Sighing, she tucked her own weapon away. "He's dead, Theo." She stayed back, not wanting to get anywhere near the body of the dead hitman and his pooling blood. Or the other bodily stuff. Ugh. Half his head was gone and she really, really didn't want to be near it.

Even though Theo had told her he'd be bringing in a cleaning crew, it was hard to see a dead body in her office. Even if the guy had planned to rape her before handing her over to likely be raped and killed. She'd seen bodies before—body parts too. Burned. Mangled. Sometimes the parts unrecognizable. Didn't mean it was something she'd ever want to get used to.

"I wish I could have made him suffer," Theo growled as he holstered his weapon.

And she could see the emotions riding him hard now as he visually scanned her, as if he was checking to make sure she was truly okay.

"I'm fine," she added, because she'd never seen him like this. Her normally relaxed neighbor—boyfriend?—looked as if a light breeze would push him over the edge. "The plan worked. Now we just need to...get rid of him." She kept her gaze averted as she stepped around her desk, giving the guy a wide berth.

While she didn't love this part of the plan, she couldn't call the police now. It was waaaaay too late for that. She'd made her bed, or decisions, as it were, and she was sticking with them. Not to mention she didn't relish the thought of calling the locals because inevitably her father would hear about it and come down here. And she didn't want to see or talk to him.

Nodding once, his jaw tight, Theo bent down and searched the guy, pulling out a simple phone from an interior pocket of the dead man's jacket. Theo used the man's thumbprint to open it, then got rid of the biometric sign-in option so it was unlocked. "He's been texting with another number. We'll check it, try to see who owns it, but it's likely another burner. There are instructions to text when the delivery is ready."

She wondered if he even realized he was growling as he spoke the last few words.

"Open your garage, Elliana," Theo's mom said quietly over the earpiece.

Oh crap, she'd almost forgotten about the other woman. "Give me a sec." Hurrying downstairs—and glad to get the hell out of there—as Theo continued searching the phone, she did as the woman asked and stepped back as she and Theo's father stepped inside.

Lorna handed her a set of keys. She was dressed casually in dark jeans and a cheery green Christmas sweater with flying reindeer, the same as her husband, Nestor. They'd told her that hiding in plain sight was always the smartest thing to do. So instead of looking like scary killers from the movies, they looked like young, fit grandparents out for a stroll in their cheeseball sweaters.

"Go next door," Lorna ordered. "In ten minutes, two people will start the cleanup process so don't worry if you see two strangers entering your garage. You'll never know they or anyone else was here. I promise."

"You don't want me to stay?"

She looked at her husband, then back at Elliana. "It's not that. It's just better if they don't see you in person. They can get kind of squirrelly about people knowing their identity."

Ah. She nodded, took the keys, and headed next door to wait.

What the heck was her life now? Someone was dead in her office, two professional cleaners were on their way to clean up said dead body—and she was pretty sure that she was in love with a hitman.

CHAPTER 15

—Morally gray is my favorite color.—

“Take the damn picture,” Elliana snarled around the gag in her mouth. She might be into watching Theo strip for her—and pleasure himself in front of her—but right about now she realized that being gagged did nothing for her.

Maybe it was because of the situation though. In a different one, maybe she’d actually like it? As she contemplated that thought, Theo just growled as he held up the dead hitman’s phone to take a picture of her “tied up and gagged” for Gillen. Or for whoever was on the end of the burner phone sending messages. She was ninety-nine percent sure it was Gillen, given the money trail of evidence, but she wanted to keep that one percent open for the possibility that there was another psycho out there who wanted her dead, just in case.

They’d staged this in a corner of Theo’s garage and she didn’t want to be lying on the dusty floor a moment longer than necessary.

“Oh sweet sugar plum fairy,” Lorna muttered and grabbed the cell phone from her son. “It’s not real, Theo. I’ll take the damn picture.” She looked at Elliana and said, “Look angry.”

Yeah, no problem. Elliana scowled at the phone as Lorna took a few snaps, then texted the pictures to the only phone number in the cell phone they'd retrieved.

Once she was done, Elliana brought her hands around from behind her and pulled the gag out. Theo crouched in front of her and was helping her to her feet before she'd even tried to stand. He held her close as if he thought she was going to fall apart.

"Theo, I'm fine," she murmured against his chest. He was being a little over-the-top about this, but he smelled good so she kept her face buried against him and inhaled.

"I just don't like thinking that this could have happened if we'd never met. That this might have been real and I wouldn't have been here to stop it."

Ooooh. Oh hell. Elliana wrapped her arms around him, very aware of his parents leaving the garage and heading into his house to give them privacy. Leaning back, she looked up at him. "It's all good. None of this is real. We're in control of all of this." She cupped his cheeks as she looked into the amber eyes of the complex man she'd fallen so hard for. "As soon as we hear back, we'll be a step closer to ending this nightmare. To putting that bastard behind bars."

He brushed his mouth over hers for a brief moment before he pulled away at a buzzing sound.

Her heart rate kicked up as she looked down at the dead guy's burner phone, read the incoming message.

It was an address in Homestead and the meeting time was five hours from now. Would probably take them an hour, depending on traffic. Maybe two.

Theo texted back a simple thumbs-up, following the same pattern that the hitter had used in previous texts. Right to the point.

"Okay, now we need to figure out where our dead guy was staying," Elliana said as she headed inside Theo's place. Or his rental, really. After being in his real home, the one with life in it, it was impossible to see this place as anything but a rental with a beige personality.

"Nestor and I will drive around this neighborhood and the adjoining ones," Lorna said as Elliana and Theo entered the kitchen to join them.

"I can just use my drone, do aerial recon a lot easier. No one will see and I'll get better angles of homes as well." She could peek in windows if necessary.

Lorna gave an approving nod as Theo picked up the keys to Elliana's place. "I'll run next door and grab it. You need anything else while I'm there?"

"Ah, I'm good." She kind of wanted to go with him—to avoid any uncomfortable conversations with his parents—but shook her head.

"You're handling all of this incredibly well," Lorna said when it was just the three of them. "You would have made an excellent hitter, especially with your explosives knowledge."

Nestor was mostly ignoring them as he peered out the kitchen window into the backyard.

"Ah, thanks." It sounded like a compliment.

"My granddaughter also loves you, so as far as I'm concerned you're already part of the family." Lorna was smiling at her widely, her expression open and kind. "For the record, I'm partial to spring weddings."

Um, what? Elliana blinked, panic bubbling up inside her at the W word. A whole lot had happened in the last few days, and yes, she was handling everything well. Either that or her brain was just waiting for the right moment to explode. And she so did not want to talk about relationship anything with Theo's mom. Who, admittedly, was incredibly nice. But it was impossible to forget that she also killed people for a living. Or she had before she'd retired. Whatever.

"My love, drop it." Nestor didn't turn around from the window as he spoke, his voice gentle.

"I'm just telling her that we like her and we're welcoming her. It's got to be intimidating to be thrown into such a chaotic situation."

As the two of them talked about her as if she wasn't there, Elliana started counting in her head, waiting for Theo to return. It was a coping mechanism she'd picked up in Afghanistan. The counting helped her to focus, to center her in most situations. It also helped when she was constructing a bomb. So her eighth grade math teacher had been right—math absolutely helped her in life.

Eighty-two seconds later, Theo strode back in the door, that relaxed grin on his face as he carried Luna, her favorite drone.

And she could breathe again. Elliana was already off the stool and grabbing his hand to drag him out the back door onto the patio before he could think about sitting down. "Did anyone see you?" she asked as she set up her baby.

"Nah, I jumped your fence. We're good. Is everything okay?"

"Yeah, of course." What was she going to say? *I'm worried your mom might murder me if things don't work out between us.* Because the more she thought about it, the more she realized it was a very real possibility.

"You sure?" He sat next to her as she worked the controls.

"Yeah. I mean..." She stilled for a moment. "I'm just trying to wrap my head around everything, I guess. It's been a wild few days." And his mom had just dropped the W word. Something she was definitely not going to tell him.

His expression was concerned as he watched her closely, but he nodded and simply kissed her in response.

And just like that, she melted into him for a long moment, letting the taste of him, the memory of how his mouth felt in other places, take her away. Her breathing erratic, she made herself pull back and focus on the little screen as she lifted Luna into the air.

"I'm going to do some slow sweeps looking for closed curtains, any boxes left on porches, anything that looks like someone might be on vacation." Because they were working on the assumption that the hitman had either rented a place nearby or was utilizing an empty home. Of course, he could have also murdered someone, but that was a hell of a lot riskier. Especially around the holidays when so many people were off work and school.

Not to mention there was an ordinance in most of these neighborhoods that forbade short-term rentals, so it seemed unlikely that he'd found an Airbnb to rent. If she'd been in his shoes, she'd have broken into an empty house close by to keep an eye on her place in case she returned home.

Twenty minutes later, she zoomed in on a house that had closed curtains, despite most of the homes in the neighborhood having all theirs open in the early afternoon. There weren't any Christmas lights or decorations on the house either, except for a simple wreath on the front door.

"This might be a good candidate for his temporary base of operations," she murmured, zooming out to snag the address on the mailbox. "And I recognize this place. An older woman lives here alone. Her husband died a couple years ago." Elliana just hoped the woman was visiting her kids or somewhere else and not lying dead in her home.

***

"Got it!" Elliana mentally did a fist pump as she finally cracked the laptop they'd found at the unoccupied home. Luckily there had been no dead bodies waiting for them as she'd feared. The dead hitman had been using a nearby house of a retired woman currently on a cruise in the Bahamas. Elliana had checked the woman's social media feed and found a picture posted that morning of the smiling woman holding up a drink, with the blue of the ocean behind her a perfect background.

Now she and Theo were headed to the address of a warehouse

in Homestead, where Theo was supposed to "deliver" her to Gillen. They'd left early, with his parents not too far behind. When they got close enough to the location, she'd crawl into the back and faux tie herself up.

"Find anything good?" Theo had been fairly quiet since they'd left, and she found she missed the sweet, good-natured man she'd fallen for.

But she definitely understood his stress because a low-level anxiety buzzed through her as well. They were going to try to get Gillen to admit to what he'd done on a drone recording, then turn him over to the police. Or to the Feds, she wasn't even sure.

Theo was *not* happy about this, but she'd convinced him to do it. Because jail was going to be a hell of a lot worse than death for someone like Gillen. He was going to have all his rights, everyday luxuries, stripped away. Just like he deserved.

She wanted this bastard in jail.

And they could record Gillen talking without getting Theo's face on camera since he was the one who'd be wearing the recording device.

"A file of current contracts, so yeah. And there's a ton of information to sift through." She was going through the dead man's browsing history and had already figured out where he banked. Now she was working on figuring out how many accounts he had. Because someone with his kind of profession had to have multiple accounts. "Looks like he's got some properties around the globe too, so I say we find out if he's got any family he left behind. If not, we're going to take all his money and donate it to charity."

Talk about good karma. She also pulled up Gillen's cell phone and the burner phone they'd texted. They were both moving in the same direction, both headed toward Homestead. Which meant he was dumb enough to bring his real cell phone with him.

Theo reached out and squeezed her thigh once, still too quiet for her taste.

"Is everything okay, Theo?" she murmured, placing her hand over his.

He looked slightly startled as he glanced at her.

"What?"

"Nothing. I just like when you say Theo. My name sounds good on your lips." He grinned at her, his dimples coming out to play and making her weak in the knees again.

Ooh, but now was not the time to fall down the rabbit hole of obsessing over his damn dimples. She'd do that later when it was just the two of them. She belatedly realized that he hadn't actually answered her question.

Before she could ask again, he said, "Go time."

Yeah, they were only ten minutes out. It was time to play her part. Nodding, she shut the laptop and tucked it under the passenger seat before she crawled all the way to the back. Adrenaline pumped through her, her heart rate a staccato beat in her chest, because this was it.

They'd gone over the plan multiple times but she knew anything could go wrong. Especially if Gillen had backup.

Chapter 16

—Karma is the universe's way of saying fuck around and find out.—

Theo wasn't about to walk into this place blind. The warehouse Gillen had chosen was abandoned, in a sort of legal in-between as the owner had recently filed bankruptcy. The bank owned it as an asset, but from what he could see on the screen of his dad's drone, no one was inside waiting for them.

"You see what I see." His father's stoic voice came through his earpiece as Theo remained idling in the curbside parking spot a couple blocks away.

"I should be using Luna to scout," Elliana grumbled from the back.

Theo grinned at her slightly petulant tone. "You're good where you are. We don't want to risk anyone accidentally seeing you."

She grumbled but didn't respond further.

"Can you get inside?" Theo asked his dad.

"Yeah, give me a couple minutes," his father murmured.

Theo watched the screen turn into a blur as the drone zipped around the abandoned warehouse. There were no vehicles in the parking lot, the guard booth at the main gate was unoccupied—and the windows were smashed out of the booth—and there didn't seem to be any homeless encampments around the building. From the feed, he'd seen padlocks on the two main doors so at least someone was trying to keep people out.

The drone slowed and slipped in through a high window with a pane missing. Once inside, his father moved quickly, scoping out the huge, empty space, including the rafters, looking for signs of life or some sort of setup. Other than some pigeons, there was nothing that either of them could see.

"He's pulling up," his mother said quietly. "Vehicle is an older model sedan, beige color. I ran the plate and it's not registered to Gillen, but I saw his face. It's him."

Elliana grumbled even louder from the back, but still didn't move, thankfully.

Theo hated everything about this. But before he took care of Gillen, he had to make sure that he was guilty. Everything pointed to the man's guilt, but Theo wanted to see with his own eyes. He took his job seriously, though tonight was about more than a job.

It was about Elliana, the woman he was in love with. Even if he hadn't figured out how to tell her.

"He's only ten minutes early, which makes me think he really is alone." Not some criminal mastermind. Just a rich asshole who wanted to hurt a woman he deemed not worth his time. A woman who'd had the audacity to reject him. "Are you good, Elliana?" he called out.

"Yeah, I'll put the gag in once you pull through the gate."

"Okay. We're going to wait ten more minutes, see if anyone else shows up."

Time crept by on the shell of a snail as he watched his father's drone, which was now immobile, just perched on one of the rafters. Gillen was there, outside his vehicle and leaning on the front of his sedan as he waited.

He kept looking at his watch, his impatience at having to wait clear. *Good.* Theo wanted him agitated. "I'm going to make him wait another five," he said through the earpiece.

Once the time had passed, however, he was ready to end this thing.

"Putting the gag in now," Elliana whispered, even though it was just the two of them.

The gate had been left open so he cruised through, didn't bother shutting it behind him. He wouldn't be staying long. And they'd already disconnected any nearby CCTVs, not that there were many to begin with in this neighborhood. They hadn't needed to disconnect any cameras at the warehouse because there hadn't been any working ones. So either Gillen had disconnected them or whoever previously owned this had. There had to be a link between Gillen and the owner, and they'd find it soon enough.

Once he reached the rolling door to the warehouse, he honked once, quick and light. The door rolled up and he drove in slowly, eyeing Gillen, searching for visible weapons on the man.

The door started to shut almost immediately after he'd pulled through. Theo kept driving into the cavernous space, parking his SUV about fifty feet from the sedan, with the backside of his SUV facing the front of Gillen's vehicle.

"I'm stepping out," he said quietly for Elliana's benefit only as he emerged from the vehicle. But not before turning on the small recording device, and then pulling on his balaclava. The mask was just in case there were cameras they'd missed. But he doubted it, considering they hadn't found any electronic signals consistent with recording devices emitting from the warehouse either.

Gillen looked a little startled when he shut the door, likely because of Theo's face mask—his SUV was darkly tinted and difficult to see inside so he wouldn't have seen him one way or another before.

"You have what I paid for?" the man demanded, his tone haughty. He wore casual slacks, a pastel-colored polo, Sperrys, and his light brown hair was perfectly coiffed, as if he'd sprayed it with something to keep it in place.

Silently, Theo popped the trunk to reveal an "unconscious" Elliana, her long blonde hair a messy fan around her face and shoulders, the gag and ties around her face and ankles making everything look legit. Her arms were unrestrained behind her back, and all she'd have to do was pull one tug on the rope of her ankles and the restraints would loosen.

When Gillen took a step forward, his eyes far too gleeful, Theo held up a hand. "She's still my property until you pay the rest of what you owe me." He loathed even saying the words, but kept his expression passive as he watched Gillen. The man wouldn't be able to see his face, but he could still see Theo's eyes, so he had to keep his cool.

The other man's jaw clenched, but he pulled out his phone, tapped on his screen a few times, then looked up at Theo, eyebrows raised.

"I've got to wait for my accountant to contact me." A total lie, but Theo wanted Gillen to talk first, to get him to admit to what he'd done. And he'd learned long ago that guys like this loved to talk about themselves.

Gillen glanced around nervously, but then nodded again. "Fine."

"So why do you want this one?" He jerked a thumb over his shoulder, still keeping his body in between Elliana's and Gillen's. "She was a pain in the ass to get. Would have been easier to just eliminate her."

"Because she's a bitch, that's why," he snapped. "And she's going to get what's coming to her." He grinned, the expression so evil that it took all of Theo's control not to react. "Did you sample her?" he asked, his eyes bright with excitement as he waited for the answer.

Theo paused, forced himself to play this right before he grinned slightly, gave a little shrug. "A bit. She's a fighter though. I like my women more submissive."

"She won't be fighting when I'm done with her."

Theo laughed, and though the sound felt hollow to his own ears, Gillen's body language eased so he must have been convincing.

"Stupid bitch took something from me. Something I deserve! Something she only has because of her tits and ass." He shook his head in disgust. And the "something" likely referred to the job. "She's going to find out what happens when someone tries to screw me over."

Theo nodded in understanding. He glanced at his phone, feigned looking at a text. "Money came through."

Gillen grinned, took a step forward as if to collect his prize—but froze when Theo pulled his weapon on him, aimed it directly at his chest.

Only ten feet separated them. He wouldn't miss.

"Change of plans, asshole." Elliana sat up, and he could hear her boots quietly thudding against the concrete behind him as she approached.

Theo didn't turn around, didn't want to see her face before he did what he had to do. He turned off the recording device. Because they weren't calling the cops or the Feds. Everything was too messy to involve law enforcement. But he hadn't wanted to argue with Elliana or try to convince her that his way was the right way.

He pulled the trigger, once, twice, right in the chest. And as Gillen started to fall backward, his body jerking under the impact of the metal tearing into his flesh and bone, he pulled the trigger again, hitting him right between the eyes.

Elliana gasped behind him and he holstered his weapon before turning to find her staring at him, eyes wide with shock and horror.

"Theo, we said—"

"I lied. He was never walking away from this. Ever. He wanted to kill you, paid a lot of money to make it happen. A prison wouldn't necessarily stop him. I wasn't risking your life."

Eyes still wide, she stepped back from him when he went to make a move toward her. And she might as well have gutted him for the impact of her silent rejection.

"I'm moving in." His mom's voice came over their earpieces. They had to transport the body and dump him and the vehicle soon. And they'd likely burn this place down too, for good measure.

"Elli—"

"No." Turning away from him, she stomped back to the vehicle and slid into the passenger seat, slamming the door behind herself.

Sighing, he went to open the rolling door for his mother to drive inside, his father close behind in another vehicle. And as he and his parents worked to clean up everything and transport the body to the back of the sedan, the engine of his SUV roared to life.

Right before Elliana tore out of the warehouse, the wheels squealing in anger before she cleared the rolling door.

"Damn it," he grumbled as he dropped the tarp-wrapped body into the trunk of the sedan.

"You shouldn't have lied to her." His father's tone was all casual as he stepped back, shoved his gloved hands in his pockets.

"What?" he demanded, looking between his parents. "You both knew about the plan, agreed with it!"

"Of course. It made the most sense. And she would have realized it if you'd simply talked to her about it. But you didn't even try to explain your reasoning." His mother eyed the shut trunk, said a violent curse to the dead body inside before she looked back at Theo. "You shouldn't have lied to her. Not if she's the one you want to spend the rest of your life with. Partnerships have to be equal."

Yeah, he knew that. Absolutely knew it. But he'd make the same decision again to keep her safe. "I need—"

His father glanced down at a buzzing sound, frowned at his phone. When he looked up, Theo knew something was wrong.

"I just got an alert. Gillen's contract opened up. What the hell!"

An icy dagger slid through his rib cage. If someone else had picked up the contract, Elliana was still in danger. "How is that possible?"

"He must have had it set to reopen if he didn't manually check in or cancel it out by a certain time. It would ensure she ended up dead even if something happened to him—that's got to be it. Because this one is for a kill only and it's only half of what he'd originally offered. This is a backup fail-safe."

Fuuuuck. They'd had clients who'd done this before, but he hadn't expected it from someone like Gillen.

His father tossed him the keys to his SUV. "Go. We'll take care of the body. And I'll cancel out the contract."

Theo raced out of there without another word. Elliana only had a few minutes head start on him. He was going to get his woman. And if someone else was dumb enough to come after her, they were going to die too.

He'd burn down the entire world for her.

CHAPTER 17

—If my life were a movie, my bad decisions would be the twist ending.—

Elliana was still fuming by the time she made it home. She didn't have her phone, which was just as well, because she wouldn't have taken a call from Theo anyway.

Not after what he'd just done, the lying bastard.

After parking his SUV in his driveway, she headed across his yard, then hers, and punched the inflatable Grinch once before marching up to her front door.

It took a couple tries for her to get her door open because it was dark out and her hands were shaking so bad. And as she stepped inside, she realized her cheeks were wet. She couldn't believe she was crying.

Angrily, she swiped at her tears, even as she realized her phone was still next door at his place. *Damn it.*

She didn't have a key but he'd given her the code to his front door at least.

"Stupid, stupid," she muttered to herself as she hurried up the stairs. She needed to find the code he'd written down for her, even as she cursed herself for not memorizing it. But she needed her phone. And to pack a bag, because she absolutely was *not* staying here tonight.

She couldn't talk to Theo, didn't want to look into his handsome face, to experience that betrayal all over again. She swallowed hard as she hurried into her office—which was shockingly pristine—and started rummaging around on her desk—but froze when it registered that she hadn't needed to turn off her alarm system.

She knew she'd set it. It had been the last thing she'd done on her phone before she'd left her cell on Theo's countertop. She hadn't wanted to bring it with her for a whole lot of reasons, and now... Ice trickled down her spine as she thought of the implications.

Was someone in her house right now? She had a Taser, but it was in her bedroom, along with her pistol.

Damn it, damn it!

Think, think, think.

If someone was in her house, they'd heard her moving around already because she hadn't been quiet. Reaching into her top desk drawer, she pulled out the block of C-4 she'd tucked away before, then got to work with the det cord, her fingers moving deftly after years of experience. Then she pulled out a letter opener and eased back to the big window that overlooked Theo's house.

As she shoved it open, she saw movement behind her, reflected in the window. Turning, she moved on instinct, grabbed the nearest lamp and ripped it out of the wall.

No need to be quiet now.

Screaming in the hopes that one of her neighbors heard her, she threw the lamp at the hooded, masked figure advancing on her.

He tried to duck out of the way but it glanced off the side of his head. As he moved, she saw something long and slender in his hands. *What the hell...* This freak had a garrote?

Hell no, she wasn't letting this guy strangle her to death. *No, no, no!* She'd blow them both up before she let that happen—but she planned to get the hell away from here before she blew his ass up.

Glad he didn't appear to have a pistol or other type of weapon, she jumped up on her desk with the intention of escaping out the door. If she could get outside, she could definitely outrun this guy—and detonate the C-4 in the process.

Grunting, he dove at her, tried to swipe her legs out from under her, but she was a hair faster.

She made it off the desk and reached for the only thing she could grab—the four-tiered bookshelf.

Glad she'd been lazy and hadn't secured the thing to the wall, she heaved it at the guy as he made it around the desk.

"Bitch!" he snarled as it slammed into him.

Unfortunately she was on the other side of the sudden barricade she'd made and couldn't get to the door without going through him. She briefly contemplated taking him on, but without knowing what his training was she wasn't getting involved in close-quarter combat with an unknown. Hell no, she was going to live to see another New Year.

As he struggled to get it off him, she hurried to the window, glanced down at the bundle of blow-up penguins outside. "Screw it," she muttered as she hoisted herself through the window and jumped for the happy, smiling penguin family wearing Santa hats.

As she slammed into them, she clutched onto the biggest one, holding on as it deflated under her weight. Fear punching through her, she looked up to see the masked man at the window, a knife now in his hand.

She screamed "Fire," hoping to get attention, this time even louder as she rolled off the penguins and onto the grass. Kicking out, she accidentally dislodged the stakes holding the penguins in place as the man started to crawl through the window after her.

Even though she hated to do it, she pressed the button on the detonator and ducked as wood and plaster shattered in a huge explosion above her.

She cried out as something thudded against her back, but shoved up at the sound of fire crackling, glanced behind her to see that the asshole had landed on the penguins. His shirt was on fire though so he was a little messed up at least. Too bad he wasn't dead.

"Come on!" she shouted at the universe as she pushed to her feet and sprinted down the length of her yard, her long legs eating up the distance between her and the SUV she'd left parked. As she reached the end of the fence delineating their properties, another SUV suddenly appeared and jerked to a halt in front of her yard.

Theo! Relief punched into her.

She was vaguely aware of people coming out of their houses around her, but had to tune them out as she fought for survival.

Diving for the inflatable snowman, she yanked out one of the stakes and brandished it as a weapon just as Theo jumped from the SUV. "Killer!" she shouted, hoping he'd understand as she turned and swung at the oncoming attacker, wielding the stake like a blade.

Hauling back as the assailant dove at her, she swung hard, slamming him in the shoulder even as she screamed obscenities at him. This asshole thought he could break into her home, kill her. *Hell no!*

He slashed out with his knife but she dove to the side, narrowly missing a slash to her stomach.

"Duck!" Theo shouted from somewhere to her right.

She didn't question the order, just threw herself onto the ground with blind trust as she heard *pop, pop, pop.*

Before she could move, the man fell next to her, his eyes wide and unseeing, a bullet hole in the middle of his forehead, the top of his mask torn away under the impact of the bullet.

"Elli!" Big hands grabbed her shoulders, pulling her to her feet, and she was aware of two other neighbors from across the street hurrying toward them.

Too little, too late.

"I've called the police!" Ms. Alice called out to them.

"Stay back," Theo shouted as he wrapped his arms around Elliana. "Was he working alone?"

"Yeah," she rasped out through a shuddering breath, not wanting to turn around and see the destruction to her house. "Or I think."

"Fire department's on the way too," Alice called out.

Elliana nodded her thanks to the older woman as she clutched onto Theo. He was here. He'd come, he'd shown up when she'd needed him. Even after she'd stormed off. He was here, protecting her once again. Her throat tightened with a ball of emotion.

"Too bad I blew up half my house or we could have called your cleaners to get a bulk discount on bodies," Elliana murmured only loud enough for Theo as he held her upper arms and scanned her for any injuries.

Theo stared down at her, let out a strangled laugh as he gently took the stake from her hand. She hadn't even realized she was still holding it. Part of her wanted to hit him with it for what he'd done. But it was impossible to hold on to her anger when he just kept showing up and saving her life.

"I'm not letting you go again. If you're angry, you stay and we fight it out," he demanded, his hold around her tightening.

Everything seemed to funnel around her, as if she'd just come out of a firefight. She held him back just as tightly as the reality of the night crashed in on her, threatened to drown her. She didn't bother to look behind her because she knew the guy was dead. And that her house had suffered a lot of damage.

"You're going to have to answer questions," she whispered, keeping her arms tight around Theo. She might be angry he lied to her, but she didn't want him in trouble, would do everything she could to protect him. "The cops will take your weapon too, even if this was clearly self-defense."

"It's fine. This is a registered one. Are you sure you're okay?" He was looking down at her again, fear haunting his expression.

"I'm okay." Or she would be. "I'm just pissed this happened at all." She should have been paying more attention when she'd gotten home, should have realized the alarm was off.

"Do you have the detonator?"

"Yeah, in my pocket."

Theo slid his hand into her pocket, plucked it out. "Go distract Ms. Alice. I'm going to plant this on the dead guy. Make this as neat as possible."

"Okay." She let out a shuddering breath as she half walked, half stumbled toward her neighbor.

"Oh, sweetheart." Ms. Alice might be nosy, but she pulled Elliana into a hug and gently patted her back. "It's going to be okay."

As sirens pierced the night air, she closed her eyes even as the sharpest sense of fear slid through her rib cage, punctured her chest. If Theo was arrested because of killing this guy, or if the cops figured out this guy was linked to Gillen—who they'd just killed—they could be in a whole lot of trouble.

Chapter 18

—Sometimes the family you find is better than the one you were born into.—

"How are you so relaxed?" Elliana demanded as they parked along Rebel and Weston's driveway.

"Because it's a Christmas Eve party and not a firing squad?" Theo's tone was dry as he slid out of the driver's seat.

Before she could open her door, he was there, taking her hand even though she didn't need the help. But he'd been all over her the last two days, and okay, she totally loved it. She'd tried to hold on to her anger about his lie, but then had wondered what the hell was wrong with her. This man had killed to keep her safe. More than once. Theo wasn't her lying ex. No, he was this unexpected man who went out of his way to make her smile, to keep her safe.

And there was no guarantee that Gillen would have been stopped by prison; he could have hired someone again. Could have kept trying until he succeeded. She'd just wanted him stripped of everything, but she understood why Theo had made the choice to kill him—to keep her safe.

"I mean how are you so relaxed about the other stuff."

"The state's attorney isn't going to file charges. Trust me." He paused as his phone buzzed. Then he smiled as he held it out, showed her that it was the detective assigned to the case. Talk about good timing. "Theo, here," he said upon answering.

Then, there were a lot of "yeps" and "okay," and then "have a great Christmas." When he hung up, she already knew the answer, but relief punched through her when he grinned.

"Told you. I'm good and so are you. Everything's fine. Now we can enjoy Christmas."

"So, they're not pressing charges?" Because she needed all the details.

"Nope."

"Well what else did he say?" she demanded.

"They haven't been able to find out much about the guy, but your cameras and alarm were disabled around the same time, about half an hour before you got home. The guy had multiple weapons on him, including the knife and garrote you saw." He gritted his teeth at that, took a steadying breath before he continued. "And his prints are in the system from a long-ago cold case. A double homicide of a senator and his mistress. They're blaming him for blowing up your house too. This is a very neat case for them and they're closing another one."

"Jeez," she murmured. She was glad it was over though. Even her dad had reached out, via text, because he'd heard about the attack and explosion. It was all over the news right now, but he'd have heard anyway. She hadn't responded to him yet other than to say she was fine. Wasn't sure if she would say more anyway. She'd started to create a family that cared for her, would do anything for her.

"Yep. No one cares that this guy is dead. We did them a favor."

Elliana looked around the huge front yard and long, winding driveway of Rebel and Weston's mansion. "What about the other thing?" Because he'd been pretty quiet about it the last two days and she hadn't wanted to talk about it.

Theo pressed her up against his vehicle, caging her in. "He's gone. For good. And the contract is officially closed out. And I know I said it before, but I shouldn't have lied to you. I'm sorry. I should have told you my concerns and explained why I was doing it."

She slid her hands up his chest, rested them lightly on the hard expanse of muscle. "Please don't apologize again. I...just need transparency in the future. Not that I want something like this to happen again."

"No promises," he murmured. "But if someone threatens you after this, I'll be honest about what I'm going to do to them."

"I...don't know how to respond to that."

"Just say you love me and call it a day."

She blinked up at him, all the air sucked from her lungs. "What?"

"I love you, Elliana Reed. So put me out of my misery and tell me you love me too." The way he looked at her with those tiger eyes, as if he was actually unsure of her answer, pierced her heart.

She'd been hurt that he'd lied to her, but that had been based on bullshit from her past. Based on a man who'd lied simply to hurt her.

That wasn't Theo. Theo had lied to keep her safe. And the truth was, there was no good way to have turned in Gillen after what he'd done. It would have put way too much of a spotlight on Theo and his family, since they'd been there. They wouldn't have had a good way to explain how she'd found Gillen's bank accounts either. And hurting Theo or his family was the last thing she ever wanted to do. She'd just desperately wanted that asshole in prison.

"I love you too," she said. And as she said the words, it was like pressure released inside her. She'd been holding on to those words and hadn't even realized it. Because she loved this man so much it hurt.

Grinning, Theo crushed his mouth to hers and she leaned into him, wrapped her arms and legs around him—only to be interrupted by someone clearing their throat.

Blinking, she pulled back to find Rebel and Weston staring at them. Grinning.

Well, Rebel was grinning. Weston was staring with something a lot like shock.

Elliana let her legs drop from around Theo and adjusted her stupid Christmas sweater he'd convinced her to wear.

"You must be Theo." Rebel stepped forward, her hand out, still grinning as she looked between the two of them. "And since you got Elliana to come to this party, and to wear a Christmas sweater, I think we're keeping you."

"Elli loves Christmas," he murmured, shaking Rebel's hand, then Weston's.

Rebel's eyes widened slightly. "*Elli*? Oh, I love the two of you together already." She linked her arm through Elliana's, and Elliana found herself tugged along toward shouts of laughter and a cheerful rendition of "Rudolph the Red-Nosed Reindeer." "I'm so happy you're here. It wouldn't be a party without *Elli*."

"You're not going to start calling me that." She glanced over her shoulder to see Weston sizing up Theo, which didn't surprise her at all. She had a lot of explaining to do, and Theo was going to have to earn Weston's trust. "And help Theo with the stuff in the car," she called out to Weston. Because her man had baked a lemon loaf, bought an expensive bottle of wine and had even picked out presents for the dirty Santa game.

Theo grinned at her, and even in a ridiculous sweater with a dancing moose and Santa he *still* managed to look at ease—and like the sexiest man who'd ever walked the earth.

"So how are you doing after that break-in and everything that happened with your house?" Rebel asked as they headed up the driveway. "And for the record, you're always welcome to stay with us until everything is fixed."

"I'm doing good. And I'll be staying at Theo's until the damage is fixed, but I seriously appreciate the offer." She could have just rented a nice place, but Theo wasn't having any of that. And okay, she didn't want to rent some place either. She'd loved waking up in his bed the past two mornings.

"I have a feeling you'll be staying there forever," Rebel whispered.

Butterflies launched inside her at her friend's words, but she just shook her head. She didn't want to get ahead of herself or jinx anything. "So, I have a huge favor to ask you. Like huge, huge. And feel free to say no."

"Well, what is it?" Rebel demanded as they entered the foyer to be greeted by one of her dogs, a mutt named Jupiter who was currently wearing an ugly Christmas sweater.

He gave Elliana a mournful look.

"I get it, boy," she murmured, bending down to scritch behind his ear. "My sweater sucks too."

He nuzzled her before moving over to Theo and sniffing him and the presents. As the two greeted each other, Elliana stood back up to ask Rebel for her favor. "Theo's niece is a huge fan of yours, and I was thinking that maybe—"

"You want me to come over and be her Christmas present? I'm totally in."

Elliana's mouth fell open. "Uh, I was thinking more like stop by sometime over the Christmas break or in the new year but *yes*, if you don't mind. I will literally be a hero for all time."

"You don't have to impress her," Theo murmured as he moved up next to her. Without pause, he wrapped his arm around her shoulders and tucked her up against him in the most protective way. She loved the way he always needed to be touching her, because the feeling was definitely mutual.

She gently elbowed him. "He's just saying that because I'm about to blow his number one uncle spot out of the water."

Rebel's grin widened. "I'll be there, just let me know where and what time. We actually have really chill plans for tomorrow since we're hosting the party tonight."

Weston handed over a couple of the bags to Elliana before he scooped up Jupiter like he was an actual baby as he shut the door behind them. "I'm going to take this one back to our room. I think he's had too much excitement for the evening."

Rebel kissed him once before she ushered Elliana and Theo into the kitchen, where so many of Elliana's friends and coworkers were already waiting.

Warmth flooded her chest as they were surrounded by friends. Friends who'd become family in the last couple years.

For so long, she'd tried to keep herself from getting hurt emotionally, which she'd realized in the last couple days was impossible. And if there was no risk, there was no reward. Something she had no problem recognizing in her professional life. But she'd been trying to play it safe with her personal life. The one that actually counted.

Looking up at Theo to find him staring down at her with nothing but love in his eyes, she realized that he was the greatest reward ever. Maybe the universe had given her this weirdo to make up for the absolute asshole she'd fallen for before.

Whatever the reason, she wasn't going to screw this up. "I really do love you," she whispered. "More than I thought was humanly possible."

In response, he kissed her again, just a light brush of his lips over hers before they were greeted by Van and his date for the evening.

But there was a promise of more in that kiss. A lifetime of more.

CHAPTER 19

—Merry Christmas!—

Stretching, Elliana opened her eyes to find Theo sitting next to her, a mug of coffee in hand, watching her. And something smelled really, really good. "Morning," she murmured, pushing the covers off.

"Morning." He handed her a mug of coffee as she struggled to sit up.

"What's that smell? Did you cook?"

He snort-laughed. "Nope. My sister's oven is out so she's downstairs in the kitchen working on Christmas lunch."

"Oh wow, maybe we should help—" Breaking off, she stared at the huge ring on her left-hand ring finger. Blinked. Wait, was she still asleep?

"You're awake," Theo murmured.

Had she said that aloud? "What is this?" It took a moment before she could tear her gaze away from the glittering pink rock.

Looking quite smug, he shrugged and leaned back against the headboard. "It's exactly what it looks like. A pink diamond—an engagement ring. Custom made just for you. Because you're one of a kind."

She sputtered for a moment even as his sweet words rolled over her.

"You can't... What!"

"You're going to marry me, so I figured what's the point in asking?" Again with that smug smile. And those dimples, the ones that could pretty much make her agree to anything. Including marry him without an actual proposal.

"I... You..." She looked down at the ring again, admired the way it sparkled in the beams of early morning sunlight. "It really is a gorgeous ring." Something she never would have picked for herself, but somehow it was absolutely perfect.

"So is that a yes?"

"Theo, we just met!"

"That's not true. We've been engaging in foreplay for almost a year. And we've dealt with more than most people do their whole relationships. I know how you react under pressure and it's hot as hell. And I've seen how you are with people when no one is around. You're it for me, Elliana. I've never lived my life according to anyone else's rules and I don't plan on starting now. So I don't see the point in waiting when I love you. When you're the most amazing woman I've ever met. I'd be insane *not* to want to marry you."

As his words rolled over, she swallowed back a lump of emotion. "Okay," she whispered.

"Okay...what?"

"Okay, I'll marry you."

Dimples on full display, he leaned forward and claimed her mouth with his. Then he claimed her body for a long, long time.

***

"This is the best Christmas I've ever had. Aileen and Nestor, thank you so much for cooking everything. You did an amazing job," Elliana said to Theo's sister and dad, the two who'd done the majority of the cooking while everyone else played soccer in the backyard.

Well, she'd sipped wine and watched the sports because Theo's family and neighbors were all really competitive. Way too intense for when she wanted to relax and enjoy the incredible vino.

"Yes, my loves, you two deserve to go rest." Lorna stood from the table, smiling at the two of them. "We'll clean up while you go kick your feet up."

At that, everyone—including neighbors, aka other hitmen, or hitpersons—all stood and started clearing off everything with military precision. But when she tried to join in, Lorna shooed her off.

"No, no. You're a guest today. But next year I'll let you help." She winked at her as she nudged her out of the way.

"Come on, that's not fair." Dante, a very large man who Elliana was pretty sure was totally obsessed with Aileen, grumbled.

"Sulking isn't attractive, Dante." Lorna patted his scruffy cheek once before pointing out that he should pick up more dishes.

"Enjoy this while it lasts," Theo murmured, kissing the top of Elliana's head. "My mom loves putting people to work, but she *really* likes you."

More warmth spread through her at her fiancé's words. *Fiancé*. That was still a shock to her system, one she wasn't sure she'd get used to anytime soon. Not that Theo seemed to be planning a long engagement. "Okay, I think Rebel is going to be here soon anyway," she whispered as she pushed up from the dining room table.

Rebel and Weston had been invited to a lunch with their friends Molly, Tag, and their kids, but were stopping by Theo's for the big surprise for Nessa.

"You're going to be Nessa's favorite after this," Theo said on a laugh.

"What are you two talking about?" Dante was back in the dining room, frowning. "I'm Nessa's favorite." And he was deadly serious about it too. Oh, he had it so bad for Aileen.

"Please," Theo tossed out. "I don't know what planet you live on, but I'm the favorite."

"Pretty soon it won't matter because I will bury you both with my awesomeness." Elliana grinned at the two of them.

Dante gave her a disbelieving look, but she kept smiling because she was sure of her victory, and headed for the lanai to find Nestor and Aileen both relaxing. "Can I join you?"

"Sure." Aileen grinned, scooted a chair out for her to sit next to her as they watched Nessa in the pool. The ten-year-old had left the table before everyone else and had run out to swim, saying she was tired of soccer and that she wasn't watching "dumb Christmas movies on TV" anymore.

A girl after Elliana's own heart, and as soon as her stomach settled, she'd be getting in the pool too. Being able to actually swim on Christmas Day was one of the perks of living in Florida.

"So, I have a present for Nessa that maybe I should have told you about," she said to Aileen. She really needed to get used to this whole aunt thing and remember to talk to Aileen first. Maybe she was more like Theo than she wanted to admit.

"Oh my gosh, you didn't have to do that." But it was clear that the news pleased Aileen.

Before she could respond, her phone rang in her hand and Elliana answered after a quick apology. "Hey, are you here?"

"Yep, just parked."

"Okay, give me a sec. I'll meet you out front." After she hung up, she said, "I'll be right back."

Thankful that no one else was around because it seemed they were all in the kitchen, Elliana ushered her two friends in, giving them both big hugs. "You're amazing for doing this."

"Of course. I'm so excited to make a little girl's Christmas—oh my god! Let me see that ring!" Rebel grabbed her hand, her eyes going wide. "This thing is stunning."

"We'll talk about it later. Come on," she said, trying to hush Rebel. She didn't want the others to overhear.

But it was too late. Theo, his mom, and Dante had come out of the kitchen, some of the others with them.

Lorna's mouth dropped open, which made Elliana smile. She hadn't thought anything could surprise the badass woman.

"This is Nessa's Christmas surprise," Elliana said, dragging Rebel to the backyard before making introductions.

She left Theo to introduce Weston to the others as they hurried out back.

"Nessa, I have a Christmas surprise for you," she called out as she and Rebel walked out onto the lanai.

Nestor's expression didn't change but Aileen's mouth dropped open just as her mother's had, and she let out a little gasp.

"Hi," Rebel said with a smile at both of them.

But then a scream pierced the air. "Oh. My. God!" Nessa screamed again. "You're Rebel Martinez! And you're at my uncle's house!"

Rebel blinked, then grinned at the little girl who'd scrambled out of the pool and was dripping wet. "Yep, last time I checked."

"I'm your biggest fan. Absolute biggest! Elli said she knew you but I thought she was exaggerating."

"So, am I the coolest relative or what?" Elliana demanded. Because yes, she needed it validated—the others needed to know that she was in first place and would never be dethroned.

"You're the best ever!" Nessa screamed, apparently all she was capable of doing at the moment.

Elliana glanced over her shoulder at Dante and raised an eyebrow triumphantly as he came to stand on the lanai, moving in close to Aileen.

"You want to see me do cannonballs?" Nessa asked Rebel, jumping up and down excitedly.

"Sure. Can I grab a drink first?"

"Your man can bring you one," she said with authority, grabbing Rebel's hand as she stared up at her with wide, adoring yes. "Elli says that a good partner should take care of you."

Elliana couldn't smother a laugh.

"Go, I've got your drink," Weston murmured, kissing the top of Rebel's head with a laugh as Nessa dragged her off to the pool.

"Did you hear that, Dante? I blew you out of the water. Probably for all time."

"It's sexy when you gloat," Theo murmured, nipping her earlobe.

"I'm glad you think so, because it's something you'll have to get used to—since I win all the time." She leaned into his kiss, only pulling back and laughing when Rebel stripped off her dress to reveal a bathing suit underneath and cannonballed into the pool with Nessa.

Dante just rolled his eyes and headed back inside, the handsome hitman clearly annoyed at her triumph. He'd have to get used to her awesomeness too.

Aileen was staring at her, eyes wide. "I can't believe you did this. I can't..." Tears glittered in her eyes as she pulled Elliana into a tight hug. "Thank you so much. You've made my little girl's ultimate dream come true."

Feeling only a little awkward, she hugged Aileen back. "She's a good kid."

"You all spoil her," the beautiful redhead murmured, but there was no heat in her voice, just muted laughter as she stepped back, wiping at a few errant tears.

Nestor patted Elliana gently on her shoulder before heading inside, and she figured that was all the approval she was going to get from the quiet man. Well, she would take it.

She would take all of this. This big, loud family she was claiming as her own. They looked nothing like the one she'd imagined once upon a time. Not even in the same universe as she'd imagined, but it turned out they were a hell of a lot better than her imagination, thankfully.

"I love it when you smile." Theo wrapped her up in his arms, pulled her close.

And she never got tired of being held by him, of holding him right back. "I have a lot of reasons to smile lately."

The biggest one was in her arms. "Merry Christmas."

"Merry Christmas, baby."

Dear Readers

If you'd like to stay in touch and be the first to learn about new releases you can:

Check out my website for book news: https://www.katiereus.com

Also, please consider leaving a review at one of your favorite online retailers. It's a great way to help other readers discover new books and I appreciate all reviews.

And an extra note for my word nerds: I went back and forth on whether to use hitman or hit man. The various dictionaries don't agree and colloquially, it feels like hitman is used more than hit man. So I went with hitman since it's more visually appealing to me and stuck with it. I know that 95 percent of you won't care about this at all, but I also know that I've got some readers who are word nerds like me. And it's always fun to share about my process.

Happy reading,
Katie

ACKNOWLEDGMENTS

As always I owe thanks to Kaylea Cross, who read as much of this as possible before heading off on her big adventure! And I'm incredibly grateful to Sarah Romsa, for reading an early copy—and all the other things you do that amount to personal therapy. To my editors Kelli Collins and Julia Ganis, you both laughed in all the same spots per your notes so my work as a writer is done! Thank you both for your valuable insight and words of encouragement. I'm also grateful to Tammy for thorough line edits. For Jaycee, thank you again for this cover. I had a concept in my head, but you made it a reality and it's perfect.

For my readers, who keep buying my books, writing reviews, emailing me wonderful words... you all are truly amazing. I've been writing for (I had to think about this) sixteen or seventeen years and never could I have imagined having such a long, fulfilling career. And that's because of you.

I'd also like to acknowledge my son, (who is too young to read this and isn't allowed to read any of my books ever, or if he does once he moves out, he can't tell me) who is a wonderful weirdo. The apple really didn't fall far from the tree with you. I hope you keep being you forever and don't let the world take away that bright spark that makes you so unique. And I definitely have to acknowledge that he's the one who came up with the idea for the Santa hat to be added to the cover. For my mom, who swears she's going to read this book and just skip over the spicy stuff, you've always been a support, but the last few years have been amazing, so thank you. For Piper and Jack, my two writer pups who manage to get me out of my office when they need walks, treats and sunshine, I love you both and I'm grateful to have such wonderful writing companions.

ABOUT THE AUTHOR

Katie Reus® is the *New York Times* and *USA Today* bestselling author of the Endgame trilogy, the Ancients Rising series and the MacArthur Family series. She fell in love with romance at a young age thanks to books she pilfered from her mom's stash. Years later she loves reading romance almost as much as she loves writing it.

However, she didn't always know she wanted to be a writer. After changing majors many times, she finally graduated summa cum laude with a degree in psychology. Not long after that she discovered a new love. Writing. She now spends her days writing paranormal romance and sexy romantic suspense.

COMPLETE BOOKLIST

Ancients Rising

Ancient Protector

Ancient Enemy

Ancient Enforcer

Ancient Vendetta

Ancient Retribution

Ancient Vengeance

Ancient Sentinel

Ancient Warrior

Ancient Guardian

Darkness Series

Darkness Awakened

Taste of Darkness

Beyond the Darkness

Hunted by Darkness

Into the Darkness

Saved by Darkness

Guardian of Darkness

Sentinel of Darkness

A Very Dragon Christmas

Darkness Rising

Deadly Ops Series

Targeted

Bound to Danger

Chasing Danger

Shattered Duty

Edge of Danger

A Covert Affair

Endgame Trilogy

Bishop's Knight

Bishop's Queen

Bishop's Endgame

Holiday With a Hitman Series

How the Hitman Stole Christmas

MacArthur Family Series

Falling for Irish

Unintended Target

Saving Sienna

Moon Shifter Series

Alpha Instinct

Lover's Instinct

Primal Possession

Mating Instinct

His Untamed Desire

Avenger's Heat

Hunter Reborn

Protective Instinct

Dark Protector

A Mate for Christmas

O'Connor Family Series

Merry Christmas, Baby

Tease Me, Baby

It's Me Again, Baby

Mistletoe Me, Baby

Red Stone Security Series®

No One to Trust

Danger Next Door

Fatal Deception

Miami, Mistletoe & Murder

His to Protect

Breaking Her Rules

Protecting His Witness

Sinful Seduction

Under His Protection

Deadly Fallout

Sworn to Protect

Secret Obsession

Love Thy Enemy

Dangerous Protector

Lethal Game

Secret Enemy

Saving Danger

Guarding Her

Deadly Protector

Danger Rising

Protecting Rebel

Redemption Harbor® Series

Resurrection

Savage Rising

Dangerous Witness

Innocent Target

Hunting Danger

Covert Games

Chasing Vengeance

Redemption Harbor® Security

Fighting for Hailey

Fighting for Reese

Fighting for Adalyn

Sin City Series (the Serafina)

First Surrender

Sensual Surrender

Sweetest Surrender

Dangerous Surrender

Deadly Surrender

Verona Bay Series

Dark Memento

Deadly Past

Silent Protector

Linked books

Retribution

Tempting Danger

Non-series Romantic Suspense

Running From the Past

Dangerous Secrets

Killer Secrets

Deadly Obsession

Danger in Paradise

His Secret Past

Paranormal Romance

Destined Mate

Protector's Mate

A Jaguar's Kiss

Tempting the Jaguar

Enemy Mine

Heart of the Jaguar

Made in the USA
Columbia, SC
23 January 2024